THE way WE DANCE

For my favorite football player ever—may you never read this book.

CHAPTER ONE

"ATLANTA'S STAR TIGHT END, *once again, let a perfect pass from Nichols go straight through his hands."*

"He has butterfingers, Tom. He also has a case of two left feet. You can't help but wonder if the two problems are connected."

"He doesn't appear to be as graceful as he was at the end of last season. If he wants to continue starting for the Jets, he's going to have to figure out what's causing his problems."

"No shit, Sherlock," I mumbled as I shut the TV off from the highlights of our first preseason workout. It was open to the media, and my fuck ups were the first thing they homed in on. Their analysis of why, and how, I may be messing up was a joke. The ex-pros that got on those shows and talked must have fucking forgotten what it was like to play.

There were highs, and there were lows, and sometimes there wasn't any explanation. Especially from someone sitting behind a desk wearing a fucking bow tie.

"Why didn't he catch that?"

"Well, it wasn't because I wasn't fucking trying," I spoke out loud to no one as I slammed the remote down on my coffee table.

Standing up, I started pacing my apartment, anger coursing

through me. I had never been known as someone who could keep my emotions in check. I flew off at the handle and used my fists when I felt the need to do so, and it seemed to be getting worse as the season slowly got underway.

We were reporting to camp in two weeks. Practices were designed to knock off the rust. Yet, for some reason, the media liked to take their little insights and run with them. Unlike previous years, I was taking their words to heart, letting them invade my psyche and course through my veins.

Probably because they were right.

Shaking my arms out, I continued my pacing, trying not to put another hole in my walls. So far, I had been lucky and hit drywall every time I felt the need to punch something, but eventually, I was going to hit a stud and break my fucking hand.

There was a reason I was the league-leading tight end. I was big, tall, and fearless. Even if I was struggling, my reputation should have been enough to keep me on top. Unfortunately, when my fucked up past decided to show back up in my life, it made me angry that I wasn't strong enough to kick it out and turn a blind eye. I welcomed it back in like a lost little boy, and with it being time to play ball again, I needed it to go the fuck away. There was no other way to balance my past and my present.

I was never returning to being a kid on the streets.

Never.

Football was my ticket off the streets, and pretty much the only thing I knew how to do. I grew up with a slut of a mom, and a drugged-out dad that went missing on us when I was nine. My brother and I raised ourselves, and we both had determined we would be dealing on the streets of our neighborhood for the rest of our lives. We were okay with that, and we were fucking good at it by the time we were in high school.

Then, during my sophomore year, I got into a huge fight with a guy from another neighborhood. We didn't walk around in gangs, but that was about as close as it got, and when he found out my brother was dealing on his street, he wanted to take it out on me.

My brother, who was four years older than I was, had already graduated the year before and was bigger and better than that motherfucker would ever be. So he took the weak way out and tried jumping me when he knew my brother wouldn't be around.

He was a fucking coward, and a fucking fool, because I beat his ass so bad the cops had to be called. I was arrested and only able to be released on the condition that I returned to school and joined the football team. They thought it would be a good way to focus my anger and keep me occupied and out of trouble.

And it fucking worked.

Coach was a badass that didn't take my shit. By the time I graduated, he had become the dad I didn't have, but so desperately needed. He kept me in line, fed me when needed, and ensured I was always on time to practice.

When college scouts started creeping around, I pushed them away. I wasn't going to leave my brother, and I sure as fuck wasn't going to become a boy scout just to stay on a team. Plus, I hated school. Four more years of it sounded like torture.

Coach didn't let me cop-out though. He pushed and pleaded until I agreed to visit a few colleges on his dime. What I found when I got there was not what I expected.

Gorgeous women were everywhere, and the educational side all but guaranteed athletes a pass. I was courted and cared for better than I had ever been in my entire life. The appeal hooked me, and despite my brother getting pissy about it, I signed with the number one college in the nation on a full-ride scholarship as a defensive end.

My college days were when I learned I could actually catch a ball. It wasn't long before my 6'5, 260-pound body found himself lining up on the offensive line as a jumbo tight end. The other teams thought it was a fluke, that I was just there to block, but when the quarterback threw me the ball, I caught it with the tips of my fingers, and my fate was sealed. I was the starting tight end for the rest of my college career, and got drafted in the first round of the NFL draft a year before I was set to graduate.

Tight ends didn't get drafted in the first round—not usually—but Atlanta took that chance, and I hadn't let them down in my six years in the league.

Atlanta's coach became another figure in my life that I looked up to. He was fairly young in terms of being an NFL coach, but he was smart, and dedicated. He gave me insight, kept me connected, and he didn't waste time when he saw me struggling. He got in my face and told me exactly what I had to do to stay on his team.

One of the main things he wanted was for me to keep my nose clean and away from my hometown. Away from my parents and brother.

And I did.

For six years, I stayed in my lane, made Coach proud, and made sure there was a big black line between the old me and the new me.

How was I supposed to know my brother and our old friends would show up to spend the summer in my world? How was I to know when they asked to stay at my place for a few nights that they wouldn't leave? How was I supposed to know that I would be so spun up with anger and tension that I would drop every fucking ball thrown my way?

Before Coach found out, and assumed I was back in my old shit, I needed to kick my brother and his friends to the curb. So far, I had avoided falling under their pressure to get me to do something that would be a detriment to my career. Most of the time, we went to 678, and I kept myself busy dancing with the ladies.

Coach told me dancing was a good way to keep myself loose

and my feet light. Somehow, after dancing all summer at the club, I was heavy-footed and tight.

I blamed my company.

"Yo," my brother yelled as he and his two friends, Marcus and Devon, walked in from God knows where.

"Hey," I mumbled, stopping my pacing to see them making themselves at home. And why wouldn't they? They had practically moved in.

"What ya been up to?" Mike asked.

"About to head to the training facility. Where have you three been?"

They all looked at each other, clearly debating if they wanted to tell me. Until I was in it with them, they wouldn't tell me anything.

"Don't worry about it, forget I asked. Just do me a favor," I broached the subject while I was angry enough not to care what happened. "You three need to get out. I start camp soon, and then the season. I need to focus."

"The fuck?" Mike yelled. "You gonna kick out your blood?"

"Yeah, I am. The summer was fun, but it's time to get real."

"Real?" he scoffed and looked at his friends. "We are as real as it gets. Or did you forget where you came from?"

I wasn't giving him the satisfaction of an answer. I will never forget where I came from. How could I when it was standing in my living room? I turned toward my room to grab my bag and let my silence speak for itself.

When I walked back through the living room, the three of them were blocking my exit. Their arms were crossed in anger, and the looks on their faces told me my small demand was a step too far.

"You know I love you, little bro. I have always had your back," Mike pointed at me like I was twelve. "I always will. But you're fucking us out of here like I mean nothing to you."

"For fucks sake, Mike," I rolled my eyes. "Stop with the

dramatic bullshit and move. You know I love you, and I have loved having you here. But my game is shit, and I feel myself slipping. I need to get myself together."

Mike was nodding, but his chin was hard and his jaw tight. He was pissed. He didn't get it, and I knew when I got back from my workout, he would still be there, but I didn't have time to worry about it. I had a meeting with Coach and then practice, and the media was going to be there again.

"Move," I shoved Marcus, who was closest to the door.

Marcus didn't budge, instead, he bowed up in anger and clenched his fist. He was a fool to think he could intimidate me, so instead of taking my frustration out on my wall, I reared back and took it out of his face. Admittedly, it was a cheap shot that no one saw coming. Marcus wasn't a pussy, but blindsided was blindsided, and as he fell, I stepped around them, closing the door as my brother yelled, "What the fuck?"

giselle

"ONE, two, three. One, two, three. One, two, three."

I looked out among my class of inspiring ballet students and watched their form, their balance, and their focus. Eleven girls, ages five to twelve years old, and one boy who was eleven years old.

Since Sam was the only boy, I couldn't help but pay him special attention. Boys belonged in ballet just as much as girls did, but for some reason, kids that age had a hard time distinguishing that fun fact in reality. The girls tended to giggle and make fun of Sam, but to Sam's credit, he stuck with it. His parents played a huge role in his determination as well. They encouraged him to keep following his path, and to do what he loved, and Sam fed off their love and passion for him.

It's what made Sam one of my favorite students. Even when his parents couldn't afford the classes, I padded their account myself so Sam never had to miss class.

No one knew I did that, not even my receptionist. Not even Sam's parents. I would mention a grant, or some other monetary gift to the studio, and they would thank me for using some of it to let Sam continue.

Even if it did put me in a bad spot with money sometimes.

With his toes pointed and his knees bent in perfect form, I smiled at him. He had his eyes closed, and I knew he was picturing himself as the lead in Swan Lake or The Nutcracker. He was made for the stage, for the fans, for the praise. My only hope was that he stuck with it, and powered through the rough patches.

A flopping ballerina caught my eye and I turned to look at one of my five-year-olds falling to the ground.

Alycia.

She had the balance and the poise, but she was five. No amount of untapped talent could be drawn out of an undetermined five-year-old.

"Alycia, up," I clapped my hands hard and tried not to worry about her mother, who was in the viewing room on the other side of the glass wall. Alycia's mom thought that at just five years old, Alycia should be headlining Broadway. Imagine how awkward it got for me when she questioned and blamed me for her daughter's sudden outbursts in class.

I started to walk toward Alycia, and quietly beg her to stand, when Jasmine let out a scream from the middle of the class.

"Jasmine," I screeched and redirected toward her. Jasmine was one of my eight-year-old students. She was there because her grandmother made her be there. She had no desire to wear tights or do an arabesque. Poor Jasmine wanted the world to leave her alone, and most days, I couldn't blame her.

The entire class halted and stared at Jasmine as I approached her to see what was wrong. Without even having to ask, Jasmine looked toward the girl next to her and snarled, "She stepped on my foot!"

"Did not!"

"Did so!"

"Girls," I started clapping again, trying to hold in my anxiety and tears. "Girls, let's spread further apart to be safe, and try again."

When they complied, I let out a huge sigh of relief. Even Alycia got back on her feet and made more space.

Not all days were stressful. Not all days were filled with childhood antics. Most days, there was not anywhere I would rather be than in a studio, teaching the next generation of potential prima ballerinas. It was second to being on the big stage myself, but since I walked away from the tribulations of that lifestyle, I was determined to find my footing as an instructor in Atlanta.

I was the daughter of the great Galena Metrovik, after all.

People paid me to teach their kids how to be like my mother. What they didn't realize was that I was not my mother. Nor would I ever be.

I loved ballet, and I was damn good at it. But I didn't love being judged by my peers. I didn't love the outbursts of fellow dancers who thought I made it on my mother's name alone.

It happened enough that I eventually folded to the stress and abruptly dipped out of the limelight of the New York City ballet company. Then I decided to open up my studio, *Brise*, in downtown Atlanta after throwing a dart that had landed close to Atlanta. Literally, a dart. I had to get away from New York, and I had the money to do whatever I wanted for a little while. The years I spent on stage weren't necessarily lucrative, but I was a saver, and I had enough to start over.

Brise had been open for a year, and while my name alone attracted parents of little dancers, I still found myself struggling, both financially and mentally, to live up to that name. I needed a break or a change of pace. Or maybe I needed the parents of the kids not to put the hopes and dreams they had for their kids on my shoulders.

First and foremost, it was supposed to be fun. Kids would not stick with it if they were not having fun.

"Ok, let's break," I clapped again, and all of the kids tiptoed to the corner to grab their water and towels. I looked at the clock and sighed hard when I realized there were ten more minutes of class left. I turned so my back was to the parents watching in and closed my eyes.

"Miss Metro," Sam called. "Are you okay?"

Popping my eyes open, I turned toward his sweet voice. He was the one that was going to make everything worth it. He was going to power me through the next ten minutes because he was the epitome of why I was there.

"Yes, Sam. Of course, I am. I was just trying to remember the name of the next set I want to practice."

He nodded, but his eyebrows crinkled in concern. I refused to have Sam worrying over me, so I spun and clapped again, "Positions."

Everyone filed onto their marked X's on the hardwood floor and got in their ready position. I started the music and said a little prayer that the next ten minutes went smoothly.

"See you next week," I waved as the last of the parents left with their students. Once the door was shut, and I was alone, I leaned against the cool glass of the door and let it soothe me. I had to clean up and get things ready for the next day, but for a silent minute, I needed to breathe.

As much as I loved the job, it was exhausting. I always had to keep myself poised and prim, stoic and eloquent. That was what the parents of my students expected of me. That was what this industry expected of me.

With one last breath, I stepped away from the door just as it was pushed in hard, making me nearly fall into the middle of the room.

"Ahhhh," I yelled as a deep voice started yelling back.

"Shut up," he said before turning around and lowering the blinds on the door.

I was lying on the floor, scared, and looking up as the man started pacing from one side of the door to the other. He would peek out of the closed blinds every once in a while, then pace some more. There was a gun in his right hand, his finger on the trigger.

He had dark hair and fair skin, but that was the only thing I could make out. His hat covered his eyes and I could only see his profile as he paced back and forth. His clothing was nice, though. Not suit and tie kind of nice, but I knew good brands when I saw them.

Apart from telling me to shut up, he wasn't concentrating on me all. He seemed to be preoccupied with whatever was going on outside, and that thought scared me even more. Was someone chasing him?

I started to back away with a graceful version of a crab walk when my movement caught his eye. The gun immediately pointed at me and I froze in place.

"Don't move," he said deeply. "Stay still, and I'll be out of your life before you can say the word dance."

Shaking my head, I didn't believe him. He had a gun pointed at me, after all. His hat was still too low for me to see his eyes, but the scruff on his face was another feature I took note of.

He took a minute to look back out through the blinds and lowered his gun. I saw him holding something in his other hand but he accidently dropped it. When he leaned down to pick it up, he sent me a glance. Instead of grabbing the package, he rose up and walked toward me, putting his face in mine and finally giving me a glimpse of his eyes.

"Be quiet, be still," he whispered, the smell of smoke filling my senses from his breath.

I tried to nod, to agree to whatever he wanted as long as he left me alone and unharmed. The motion of my head startled him, though, because it was only a flash before his brown eyes widened with concern. With one hand on me, and one hand on his gun, he brought his head forward with force and smashed it into me.

Blackness was the last thing I saw before waking up on the floor of the studio alone. I wasn't harmed any more than the head butt, but some time had passed, and I was scared out of my mind. I lunged toward the door, locking it before sinking back down and bringing my knees to my chest.

I was not in a shady part of downtown Atlanta, but any time after dark was the wrong time to be alone. I was only at the studio that late two days a week, for the advanced classes, but in an instant, I was tempted to cancel them all.

No one worked with me during the late classes, mostly because Shannon, my front desk clerk, needed to be home with her kids. Plus, what good would it do for us both to be there?

Crawling my way to the desk, I grabbed my cell phone and dialed 911. Within minutes, I was letting the officers in and telling them what happened. An ambulance had been sent because I mentioned being hit, but after a quick scan of the damages, they deemed me okay enough to avoid an ambulance ride.

Unfortunately, they took the description of the guy, but had no other basis to go on. He didn't take anything. He didn't break anything. Aside from the head butt, I was unharmed.

Normally, I walked across the park to head home, but I asked the officer to give me a ride to make it quicker and safer. I lived in an apartment that my mother had paid for in an upscale building not far from the studio. It allowed me to avoid a car payment.

"You sure there is no reason someone would want to shake you up and scare you?" The officer asked me before I left his car.

"Nothing. I can't think of any reason at all."

"If you think of anything, give us a call. In the meantime, you may want to have a friend, or someone, stay with you at the studio. No reason to be there late at night by yourself."

Sure, I'll simply call up one of the many, many friends I had in Atlanta. All those friends I made while opening a business, and working fourteen-hour days, should pop right up out of nowhere.

Was 9:00 pm really all that late? Maybe in that area of town, but compared to New York time, 9:00 pm was early.

Things were different in Atlanta, so I nodded and closed the door as I heard him say, "We'll stay here until we see you get in the elevator."

I hadn't bothered changing out of my leotards, nor did I bother with a jacket, so I was waving the "ballerina flag" super high when a man in the lobby stopped me.

"Excuse me, ma'am?" I turned to see a well-built, well-dressed man approaching me gingerly.

Considering I had just been attacked in my own studio, I wanted to run away, and run fast. I refrained, and took solace in the fact that the cops were still outside, waiting for me to enter the elevator, and I could see their car through the floor-to-ceiling glass windows.

"Yes?"

"Are you a ballerina?"

I scoffed a little and smiled to smooth it over, "I used to be. I'm now an instructor and the owner of *Brise*."

His eyes widened with joy, and he started nodding while clearly running an idea through his brain. I started to excuse myself and tell him I had had a long day, that I was tired, and needed to go. But before I could, he laughed. "I have a huge favor to ask!"

PRACTICE WAS A BITCH. I dropped three passes, and tripped over air. I jammed my finger on my teammates helmet, and I may or may not have threatened to kill the number one quarterback in the league, Cam Nichols.

My quarterback. The one I was supposed to support and praise. The one whose passes I was supposed to catch. I could possibly look back later and say that his passes were gold, and my hands were shit, but I wasn't there yet.

I was still blaming everyone else but myself.

My brother included.

Mike still refused to leave my apartment, and I was considering the fact that I may have to get the cops involved. Either that, or I could get up and move everything while he was off doing whatever it was he did. Option B sounded more plausible since I hated cops.

"Black," I heard as I unwrapped my fists in the locker room after practice.

Looking up, I saw our assistant coach standing in the doorway. "Coach wants to talk to you."

I nodded and groaned, knowing he was going to threaten to

trade me to Arizona. Maybe he would just bench me for the preseason, but I knew he wanted to address my failures.

When I finished getting the wrap from my hands, and changed into sweats and a t-shirt, I made my way to his office. The door was open, but his head was down toward the desk, writing something, so I knocked on the door frame to let him know I was there, then walked in. He was in his track pants and a t-shirt, and his hair was a mess from throwing his hat around all day in frustration at practice.

"Sit," he huffed but never looked up at me.

Sitting down, I spread my legs and leaned back, acting as though I didn't have a care in the world.

"Here," he pushed a piece of paper across the desk, and I grabbed it, unable to read the foreign word written in his chicken scratch. There was also an address, and a name.

"What's this?" I asked, trying to say the word silently. *Briss? Brizz?*

"That's where I want you to start heading every Tuesday and Thursday until the end of preseason."

"Excuse me?" He glanced up and narrowed his eyes at me, making me regret my tone.

"That," he pointed toward the paper, "Is your ticket to the starting lineup."

My eyes squinted, and my lips snarled. Coach didn't usually talk in riddles. He was more of an "I said what I said" type of guy, so I was more confused than I was angry.

"I'm going to need more context here," I spoke with an even tone.

He leaned back in his chair and threaded his fingers together, doing a better job than I was, acting like he didn't have a fuck to give.

"That's my neighbor. She runs a dance studio. You're going to go two times a week and exercise with her."

"Coach," I smiled with disbelief. "With all due respect, you already told me dancing will help my game, and I spent a lot of time at The 678 Club dancing my ass off this summer. Didn't work."

"For fucks sake, Ty. I didn't mean grinding your dick in between the ass cheeks of women in short skirts."

"What did you mean then? Cause that is all I know to do." My arms were stretched wide, daring to question Coach with an outburst.

Coach Peyton was an ex-player, big and well-built. He was only 40 years old, and stayed in the gym as much as the players did. I had no doubt he could kick my ass if he set his mind to it. He was stern, and demanded respect. He had to when coaching at the highest level.

So when his eyes turned into slits and he crossed his arms, I lowered my attitude and sighed in defeat.

"The card has the address. Be there next Tuesday at 9:00 pm. I have already arranged the exercises you'll need to do."

Not only was Coach a man that demanded respect, but he was smart. Fucking smart. He'd led us to plenty of Super Bowls, and coached some of the best players in the world. Maybe his little game was legit. Maybe he was onto something—the key to getting me out of my slump.

"What about camp? Don't we start two-a-days on Monday?" Usually, when we checked in for our two week preseason training, we didn't check out until it was over.

"You'll be excused from anything after 8:00 pm to give yourself time to get showered and to the dance studio."

No one ever got excused from camp. Coach was going to the extreme. Was I really playing that poorly? I was in shock that he even suggested that I leave the complex.

"Look," Coach lowered his eyes to his desk while he thought about his words. "This is something I think you need. You're hardened, heavy. It's making your game suffer. Try this method without giving me shit."

Coach always got his way, and it was a right that he had earned, so I didn't argue anymore, just nodded. I wanted to do better, and be a part of the team. I wanted to make him proud. If I could do that by whatever exercises he had planned, then so be it.

"You have got to be fucking kidding me," I mumbled.

It was Tuesday evening and I was standing outside of *Brise*. Little girls in tutus and pink tights were leaving with their parents, one after the other.

A quick Google search on my phone had told me *Brise* was *"a jump in which the dancer sweeps one leg into the air to the side while jumping off the other, brings both legs together in the air, and beats them before landing."*

What the fuck?

There was no way in hell Coach would send me to ballet. Yet I double checked the address four times, and there I was.

Swiping a hand down my face, I moaned. Even moving my arms was making me cringe because I was so damn tired from practicing all day in the Atlanta heat. Now I understood why Coach insisted I shower before leaving. My football sweat wouldn't be very cute on the floor of the prim-looking studio.

Once I felt like the coast was clear, I opened the door to *Brise*, and the smell of perfume and froufrou immediately hit my senses, making me scrunch my nose. I was only in the lobby and I already hated it there.

Chairs were lined up to the right, along a huge window that looked onto a dance floor. To the left, there was a reception desk and little pink chairs lining a huge mirror.

I waited by the door, unsure if I should move in further, or wait for someone to appear. The whole atmosphere was way out of my element, and I was tempted to turn around and tell Coach I would ride the bench. No complaints either, I would keep it nice and warm for whoever was starting in my place, because fuck ballet. Anything would beat being a damn ballerina two nights a week.

Then the thought of *exercise* hit me. Coach used the word, exercise.

Exercise.

He didn't say a damn thing about dancing. Sure, he had mentioned that dancing kept players loose and flexible, but he didn't mean ballet. Not a chance.

With my back against the door, ready to run if I needed to, a woman entered the lobby through a back office door. She didn't see me, and for some reason, I didn't say anything either.

Her back was to me behind the reception counter, fumbling through papers, so I took that time to take stock of my new exercise instructor. Her dark hair was tied up in a tight bun, not a hair out of place. She was wearing pink tights and a black ballet outfit—something you would see on TV.

The ballet get-up was doing things to me that I didn't expect. For some reason, I was into it, and I watched on as she lightly moved from one thing to the next, so delicately that she looked like she was floating.

When she was finally satisfied, she turned around with the kind of grace I expected to see, but screamed as though she had been attacked. The poise and finesse that I saw in her moments before were gone. Her face was red and her right hand was stretched out, as if she were a tight end trying to defend the football on a run down the field. Her other hand was over her heart, keeping it from beating out of her chest.

"Um, hi?" I asked, unsure what else to say.

"Please leave," she spoke firmly, trying to hide her fear. "The cops have been keeping an eye on this place since last time."

Last time?

"Um, what?" She was probably scared of how mute I became, unable to speak because I was so lost by everything I had walked into.

"I have a gun," she stressed, trembling in her voice.

"Ma'am," I finally held my hands up, unsure what to call her, or what to do. "My name is Ty Black. I play football. My coach sent me here, and I am starting to think I'm in the wrong place." I reached into my pocket, grabbed the paper Coach gave me, and started to read it, but she had already lowered her hand, and her face had settled into a proper pose.

"I am so sorry, Mr. Black," she had turned right back into the graceful and composed woman I had watched gliding around a few minutes before. "I am expecting you, Mr. Peyton arranged everything."

It was as if she hadn't screamed bloody murder and demanded I leave, threatening me with the cops. Apparently, none of that had happened. She was gliding toward me, on her tip-toes, no less, with a hand out ready to introduce herself.

Some small part of me wanted to hold up two hands and yell, *"What the fuck?"* But the better part of me decided to hold off.

"Mr. Black, I am Miss Giselle Metrovik," I slowly took her outstretched hand and shook it.

"Ty," I mumbled plainly, still a little confused. "Nice to meet you."

"Likewise. Now, get those shoes off and into the studio. We can go over what Mr. Peyton asked me to help you with and start slowly."

"So, wait," I tilted my head and backed up a little. "Are we not gonna to talk about what just happened? I mean, are you okay?"

"Of course, Mr. Black, but surely you can understand how frightening it was to see a large man in the doorway unexpectedly. I apologize if I insulted you, that was not my intention."

She spoke so eloquently and registered every vowel and syllable. I didn't even hear her use a contraction, and it bothered me.

Even in fear, her poise and perfection were unmatched. I didn't know where she had come from, but something told me she was bred and groomed from the opposite side of the tracks I grew up on.

"You didn't insult me," I pinched the bridge of nose and shook my head. "Never mind."

She clapped her hands twice and got my attention, and then strolled into the studio through a couple of glass doors. "Come now."

She was not the type of woman I was used to being around. Miss Giselle Metrovik probably had more class in her left pinky than most of the women I dated combined. I found it to be both a turn-off and a turn-on.

The good news was, I wasn't there to try to get her into bed. She had been hired by Coach to help me, and even though I had no idea how the fuck her petite and uptight ass could help, I owed it to Coach to trust him. At least for a day.

Following her into the room, she turned quickly and gave me a tsk, "No no, remember? I said to remove your shoes. Always remove your shoes before stepping onto the floor, please. Socks or proper ballet flats only."

Looking down at my $250 pair of pristine athletic shoes, I started to ask her if that was fucking necessary. How was I supposed to exercise in socks? But instead, I went with it and kept reminding myself it was for Coach. For me, too, but more for Coach. He had been a mentor and I owed it to him to try.

Toeing off my shoes, I bent down to straighten my socks, and when I leaned up, Giselle was eyeing me with her hands on her hips. From the look on her face, I thought maybe I had done something wrong but she quickly clapped her hands twice and motioned for me to join her.

"First, Mr. Black..."

"Ty," I interrupted. I was called mister a lot and it never set right with me. It was too formal, and I thrived on relationships that were informal, fun, and laid back. Miss Priss was no different.

"Come stand next to me and face toward the mirror." Without acknowledging my request, she kept on. "Let me take a look at your poise and stature."

I trudged into the room, sliding my socks on the slick wooden floor, and lined up alongside her, both of us turning toward the longest wall covered in floor-to-ceiling mirrors. She stayed a few feet away from me and started telling me what she saw.

"Your shoulders are sagging, your feet are facing different directions, and your face has a scowl."

Well, fuck her too.

"Giselle," I cleared my throat, debating my response.

"Miss Metro," she interrupted while correcting me on what I should call her.

"Um, okay," I sighed. Giselle was so put together and professional, yet, when she first spoke to me, when she first saw me, she was undone and frazzled.

"Go on," she pressed.

"It's just that, so we are talking about my flaws. I get it. Anymore you wanna add?" I could hear the sneer in my own voice so I was sure she could as well. But, fuck. Was Coach paying her to degrade me for the way I stood still?

"Yes, actually. A few more," she added before turning back to the mirror.

giselle

"YOUR HIPS ARE NOT FACING FORWARD, your fists are clenched, and your biceps are too tight."

That last one may not be true. He may have just been immensely cut and strong. But I called him out anyway because it was all I could look at. The sleeves were cut off of his t-shirt and the tattoos that wrapped around his arms were intimidating.

He seemed nice enough, but I was still on edge from being attacked, and didn't know how else to deal with it other than distance and professionalism with everyone I met.

As awful as I sounded, I wasn't wrong. Ty's poise was wild and probably untamable. He was not a man used to worrying about posture and grace. I was a football novice, but I knew enough to know that those guys were amazing athletes. Most of them were naturally balanced and strong.

Not Ty.

He had probably gotten by through sheer talent for so long, but there came a time in everyone's life when that was no longer enough. Restructuring our body's needs was important as we got older.

That was where I came in and exactly why his coach asked me

for help. I had been hesitant at first. Being attacked inside my own studio didn't make me want to open it up to a stranger after hours. But then again, I was the one that set the hours.

When Mr. Peyton approached me, my first instinct was to tell him no. Absolutely no. But then he explained how special Ty Black was. His talent was endless, and he just needed something outside of the box to get him out of his stagnant regimen. It clicked that not only could I help him, but I could have him come in on the two nights I worked late.

Selfishly, I knew that meant I wouldn't be alone at *Brise*, hoping it meant I wouldn't be scared either. Even if he was a stranger.

Yet, one look at Ty Black and I screamed, losing all self-control for a moment. He looked oddly familiar, but he was a pro athlete, so that may have been where I had seen him. He was huge, tattoos all over, and his backward hat added to his formidable presence. Not to mention, I had no idea he was there, and his presence alone scared me to death.

I tried to recover quickly, and probably overcompensated by being a tad uptight. There was just no other way to move forward than to snap into business mode and conduct the evaluation I promised Mr. Peyton.

Ty needed to learn to control his form, and by doing so, he would be more effective using his natural talents on the field. By the look on his face, he wasn't informed about why he was there, or what we would be doing. Still, I pushed through, because that was my job, and the one thing I was good at.

Social skills be damned.

"Stand straight and pull your feet together, facing the mirror," I directed.

Ty was still looking at me like I had lost my damn mind, but he did as I instructed. He looked at himself in the mirror before looking back at me. "How the fuck are my biceps too tight?" he blurted.

My eyes widened at his growl and I stepped back, slightly worried he was a maniac.

"Mr. Black, calm down," I suggested before easing back into the space I was originally in. "I could be wrong, it just looks like they are constantly flexed, and that is tiresome on a body."

"They're not flexed at all," he bit back.

I knew that was most likely the case, but did I say the words out loud anyway? Sure I did. I was awkward and socially inept.

"My apologies," I said, hoping he let it go.

"That's the second time in 10 minutes you've had to apologize to me," he snarled. "You sure you know what you're doing?"

I cleared my throat and tried to remain poised, not wanting to slip in new company. "We are getting to know one another, Mr. Black. I am apologizing because I do not want to insult you. However, if I was assured that you would not be insulted, I would not be apologizing as I have not technically done anything worth apologizing for."

He broke his stance and turned toward me, hands on his hips, biceps actually flexing, "Are you fucking serious? What's your deal?"

Anger coursed through me because while I may not have been his cup of tea, nothing was wrong with me. "Should I apologize for who I am now?"

"Is it possible for you to loosen up a bit?"

"No, Mr. Black, it is not possible. I am a professional. I make a living off being a professional. I spend all day teaching grace and control. I was brought up to exude excellence."

"But you're kinda boring and snobby," he snorted, with a look of no shame for having just insulted me.

"That I am." I wasn't going to disagree. I *was* boring and probably came across as snobbier than I intended. That was what my world taught me I had to be in order to be successful.

He huffed at my agreement and turned around, shaking his head.

"Let us agree that we are two different people who can mutually benefit from one another without having to be friends, shall we?"

He turned back to me at my question and eyed me once again. "What're you getting out of this?"

I didn't want to tell him I was using him. That I was afraid to be alone. I also didn't want to mention how much I was getting paid because that was ill-mannered. But there was one more truth that I didn't mind sharing.

"Helping a tough football player for the coveted Atlanta Jets is a positive mark on my resume for future endeavors."

"Nobody is going to know I was here, *Miss Metro*," he pointed at me and lowered his brows. His sneer at my name grated down my spine but I kept myself together.

"Of course not," I whispered, lowering my head. Mr. Peyton didn't say I needed to keep Ty's lessons on the down low, but seeing Ty's anger toward people knowing, it was safe to assume the backlash wouldn't be worth the headline.

"Ya know what?" Ty started toward the door of the studio, slipping his shoes back on. "I think I'll call it a night."

"But we have not even begun," I tried to keep the panic from my voice. Ty Black was a stranger, but he wasn't a threat, and I wasn't ready to be left alone.

"Let's try again on Thursday. I think I've had all I can take tonight, Miss Priss." He opened the glass door to the studio, and I watched him leave the main door through the lobby before I could say anything else.

In order to keep myself from chasing him, I counted, but once I got to five, I ran toward the door and locked it.

"You're fine," I told myself with a whisper as I slid down the door to a squatting position. It took me a few deep breaths to feel my control come back and decide to leave.

Quickly, I grabbed my things, threw a sweater over my leotards, and slipped into my sensible shoes. Peeking out of the door, I made sure there was no one creeping around before letting myself out and quickly locking the doors to *Brise* behind me.

The cops felt that whatever happened the week before was random and unplanned, that someone probably found themselves in trouble, and chose my unlocked doors as a refuge. It made me feel like I may have been overreacting. Crime was not prevalent in that area, and even if it was, nothing was taken from the studio.

Nonetheless, after getting the doors secured, I crossed the street to head toward the park. When I was sure I had cleared the few lingering pedestrians on the sidewalks, I lowered my poise and dignity, and ran as fast as I could across the park, not stopping until I was safely in my apartment building.

ty

SOMETHING I HAD LEARNED EARLY ON WAS the importance of a second chance, and I owed it to Coach to try again with Miss Priss. As I sat in my car outside of *Brise* the following Thursday, I had to mentally prepare myself by remembering all the things Coach had done right for me. He had been a father figure since I got in the league, and without him, I would probably be headed down the path my brother took.

Trouble.

With a clear view of *Brise*, I waited in my car as everyone filed out of the studio. There was no reason to risk more witnesses than necessary. It was the same spot I had been in on Tuesday when I saw Giselle sprinting across the park. I had been sitting in my car, wrapping my head around her holier-than-thou persona, when I saw her emerge from the studio and lock the door.

She didn't know I was watching, and she couldn't have seen me from where I was parked, but I looked on as she tried looking calm and collected. But once she thought no one would see her, she ran.

It was as if all the grace she exuded was dropped, and replaced with fear. She ran like she was being chased, fearful of what was behind her. There was not another soul around, but I kept my eye on her as long as I could to be sure. I even got out of my car and walked a little to make sure she had gotten as far as she could safely. When I started my car, it still took me a bit to pull away.

The mindfuck of seeing her so studious and poised, to manic and frazzled, was confusing. Yet, kind of exciting. I wasn't mean enough to wish she lived in fear, but I was man enough to love seeing her completely undone.

Focusing back on the door, I wondered if everyone had left. One of the many things Coach taught me was that being punctual was a life skill, and being late was for the weak. So, with that in mind, I glanced at the clock and got out of my car, jogging across the street until I was in front of *Brise*.

When I opened the door, I tried being louder than the last time so I didn't take anyone by surprise. That hadn't seemed to get us off to a good start on Tuesday, and another thing Coach taught me was the importance of not repeating past mistakes.

"Hello?" I yelled when I didn't see anyone in the lobby. I walked in a little further and looked into the window where I assumed the parents sat and watched their kids do ballet. I could see the studio on the other side, and I wondered if it was a two-way window, or if there was a mirror on the other side.

I had been so flustered before that I hadn't even noticed.

Giselle had her back to the window and her head down, chin to chest. Her arms were dangling loosely by her sides before she started spinning them around. I was both curious, and intrigued, by what she was doing, so I sat down in one of the chairs and mindlessly propped my legs up on the chair in front of me.

There was no doubt that Giselle was as uptight as the PR department at a Super Bowl after-party. She was hard to talk to, and hard to connect with in the fourteen minutes I had been around her.

Still, there was also no doubt that her body was fervent and dedicated. She walked her walk, and talked her talk. Her curves and muscles were indicative of a perfect ballerina, and it had me entranced.

That was, until she tilted her head up, turned, and narrowed her eyes at me. *Definitely not a mirror.* She could see me sitting there watching.

Knowing it would piss her off, and still not able to help it, I lifted my hand and wiggled my fingers in a coquettish wave. I even managed a real smile when I could tell that she was physically trying not to roll her eyes. That would have been very unprofessional.

She didn't come to the lobby, and she didn't exactly invite me into the studio, but when her hands found her hips and one eyebrow shot up, I took that as a sign she was waiting for me to get started.

Standing up as nonchalantly as I could, not wanting her to know that for five seconds, she kind of scared me, I opened the door and remembered to remove my shoes before walking closer to where she was still standing.

"You came," she said flatly.

"I told you I would be back to start over."

"I was not sure you meant that," she sighed and walked over to a small table she had in the corner of the studio. She grabbed a phone and thumbed around for a moment before music came over the speakers in the studio.

It was a soft and whimsical song. Something I could picture at a ballet, not that I had ever been to one. Giselle walked back to me and clapped her hands in the way she did to get my attention.

"Back into the same pose we ended with the other night."

My face must have shown my confusion because I had no idea what she meant. The other night was nothing but insults.

"Stand straight and pull your feet together facing the mirror," she added, not sounding as put off as I thought she would when she had to remind me.

Doing as I was told, I looked at myself through the mirror. I had a cut-off shirt again, so my arms were on full display. Instead of shorts, I wore sweatpants, and I made sure to have a decent pair of socks on. I also had my hat on backward, and I honestly thought she would ask me to take it off, but she never did.

"Now, the idea of a physical athlete, such as yourself, taking ballet is to…"

"Hold up," I interrupted her, bringing a hand up to cut into her words. "Coach told me we were exercising, not taking ballet lessons."

"You are exercising, but I teach ballet exercises, and that is what he asked me to help you with. I am afraid I do not teach Zumba or Pilates."

Both of those sounded just as bad. I was a man, I grew up on the streets, and hit people for fun. My job was to take the heads off my opponents. It came with a mindset and toughness that couldn't be taken away with the clap of a hand. It was bad enough I was even there, but actually learning ballet? *Fuck no.*

"Listen, lady. Coach hasn't been right. He's kinda losing it a little. Can you go over for me how the hell he made you think I needed ballet lessons?"

Her lips pinched together in frustration but she nodded. "He and I live in the same building, and when we ran into one another in the lobby, he kindly asked me to give one of his players ballet lessons. I agreed, thinking that he was sending me someone who was less of a Neanderthal than he did, but the more you are here, the more I understand why this is what he chose."

"Are you insulting me again?"

"Are you insulted again?"

"You just called me a Neanderthal."

"Honestly, Mr. Black, I couldn't help it. You seem to get your 'panties' in quite a twist rather easily." She air-quoted panties and I was surprised she could keep a straight face while she did it. Air quotes didn't suit her, and I wondered if they were for my benefit, or deeply seeded into her uptight demeanor and accidentally slipped out.

Despite her bitchy attitude, I liked her bite. She seemed to be torn between uptight and savage. Some part of me wanted her to stay uptight, and the other part of me wanted to push the savage side out of her. And did she actually use a contraction?

"You know what?" I clapped twice like she did and rubbed my hands together. "You win. Let's just do this."

I pointed my feet forward and lifted my chin. I could see her unbelieving eyes in the mirror, but I kept steadfast, waiting for her to give me more instructions.

After a minute, she shook her head and decided that she would take the peace I gave her. She stood a few feet away and positioned herself the same as I was.

"There are six basic benefits of ballet that we can use to improve your football game."

Doubtful, but okay.

"Focus, flexibility, speed, strength, endurance, and balance. We will go over each in the coming weeks as we practice different poses and positions."

"Weeks?"

"Or however long it takes," she added. "But Mr. Peyton asked me to meet with you for a couple of weeks, if not longer."

"*Mr. Peyton,*" I air-quoted, "Is out of his goddamn mind."

She sighed, and I knew she wanted to come back at me with something, but she took a minute to recompose herself and kept going.

"When we are looking toward the mirror, we are looking at our audience. *We* are our audience. So we will call this our *en face* position. There are four corners to our box....."

Truthfully, I zoned out. My personal dancing box was not something I gave a flying fuck about. Nor did I care what facing the audience was called. Only when she mentioned the word *derrière* did I tune back in. Of course, that was followed with a wave of disappointment when I realized she wasn't talking about her ass but the back position of my feet.

I let her talk it out, though. I did an Emmy award-winning performance that made her think I was listening, and before I knew it, time was up.

"Okay, wow," she huffed a small laugh that was actually genuine and a little bashful. "Time flies when I talk about body positions."

"I enjoy talking about body positions, too," I smirked, making it obvious that I was not talking about ballet.

She fought an eye roll and turned around, but I did see a hint of a smile trying to creep on her face. I was a little more excited about that half-smile than I thought I would be. Who knew she was even capable of a real smile?

"We are done for the night." Her back was still to me and she was throwing some things in a bag. "I can follow you out."

I went to get my shoes and started pulling them on. By the time I did that, and got my keys and wallet from the reception area, she was standing by the door waiting to lock up. She looked nervous all of a sudden, and she didn't bother changing from her tights and small skirt. It was exactly how she left when I saw her leave Tuesday, but I thought maybe she had been in a hurry since she ran. Her clothes didn't seem suited for the sidewalks.

"You gonna change?" I asked, her face morphing back into annoyance. I guess I did sound a little judgmental, but I seriously didn't think she should be walking home in *that*, especially so late. Since I knew she lived in the same building as Coach, I knew she lived across the park and most likely didn't drive.

"No time," she quipped. "I have to hurry home."

Dipping my chin, I accepted her answer. It was not my place, not my problem. Walking toward the door, I gave her a curt nod goodbye. She left right behind me, and locked the door quickly.

While I walked to my car, I noticed her walking fast and

looking around. As much as I was keeping an eye on her, she was keeping an eye on me.

It got to the point where I was going behind a building and she was continuing through the park, so I lifted my hand in a lazy wave, acknowledging that I saw her, and was bidding her good-bye. She did the same right before I disappeared behind the building.

Something made me stop, though. I worked my way back the six steps that I had taken and peeked around to look toward the park. Sure enough, Giselle was sprinting down the sidewalk, and looking over her shoulder to make sure no one was following her.

She definitely had to hurry home, but she was scared. We were in a fairly safe part of town, but walking alone, and late, was daunting. Especially for a woman, and especially one wearing as little as she was.

Once again, I had to repeat in my head that it wasn't my problem. I barely even liked the woman so I definitely didn't need to concern myself with whatever spooked her.

Despite what most women believed of me, I wasn't a cold-hearted jerk. If Giselle was spooked, then who was I not to believe she had a legit reason to be. Walking the long route to my car, I jogged a little to catch up to where I could keep an eye on Giselle. Not until she got to her building did I double back around to my car. I knew I wouldn't be able to keep an eye on her every night, and I knew it wasn't my job to do so, but just that one time, I was going to be sure.

When I walked back to my car, I grabbed my phone and started thumbing through it, ready to call Coach and tell him I was not going to be his fucking ballerina for weeks on end.

Just as I hit call, the force of running into something made me drop my phone to the ground.

"What the—" but I stopped, realizing I was looking at my brother in the fucking face.

"Hey, little bro," he laughed.

"What the hell are you doing here?"

"You mean here on this street?" He looked and pointed around aimlessly.

"No, I mean here in Atlanta. Didn't I kick you out?" Right before leaving for camp, I made it clear they had to be gone.

"Just because you told us to leave your apartment doesn't mean you get to decide where we do business."

I cringed at his words because I knew what his idea of business was and I didn't want any part of it. I didn't even want to know what he was up to. "You better have left my fucking apartment."

Mike staying in Atlanta wasn't part of the plan. I didn't want my name or family attached to any bullshit on the streets in my city.

In Atlanta, I was a God. I wasn't going to do anything to risk screwing that up. That included not dealing with my brother, not getting caught taking ballet lessons, and not sticking my nose where it didn't belong.

"We got a couple of weeks," my brother goaded, almost looking for a fight. The crazy thing was, I loved my brother. We didn't have a bad relationship, at least not when he did his bullshit somewhere else. He and I had an awesome summer hanging out and clubbing.

"Please don't do your shit here in Atlanta," I begged. I even took the liberty of weakening my voice to plead. He knew how much I loved it there. Why couldn't he leave my area alone?

"No can do, money is flowing here, LB. Me and the boys claimed these streets, and there is no going back. You aren't the only Black that loves the A.T.L."

Running a hand over my face, I shook my head as I picked up my phone. Without even bothering to look at it, I started walking toward my car again. There was nothing I could tell Mike. He would do whatever he wanted to do. My only hope was he got run off, got caught, or got bored before something major happened.

"Ty… ty…hello…" I heard my name being repeated faintly, almost as if I imagined it. I looked around but didn't see anyone else. Only my brother thumbing on his phone and leaning against the wall where we had been standing.

When I looked down at my phone to see if he was messaging me, I realized I fucked up. I connected the call with Coach before I dropped my phone and he stayed on the line. He heard the whole conversation I had just had with Mike.

Coach knew the deal with Mike. He knew he was bad news. I had promised him a million times that I had nothing to do with my brother. He had no idea Mike had been not only been in town, but had been staying with me.

He was going to think I was getting reeled back into that life, and I had to do everything I could to prove to him that I wasn't, nor would I be. I wasn't going to risk my throne in town, and on the team, for anyone.

Pulling my phone up to my ear, I decided to act like nothing had happened. There was a chance Coach hadn't heard anything, and I wasn't going to incriminate myself.

"Hey Coach, sorry. I hit call and got distracted," I cringed at my lie that wasn't a lie. "Just wanted to tell you how good…" That was as far as I made it.

"What the fuck are you doing with your brother?" Coach yelled, cutting off my words.

giselle

"TYSON BLACK IS STILL STRUGGLING *this preseason. He seems distracted, almost cursed. If you are the Atlanta Jets, you have to be asking yourself if Black is worth his impending contract extension. At this rate, I am not even sure he is worth a spot on the bench this season."*

It was Sunday, and while I normally didn't spend my Sundays watching sports, I considered watching videos of Tyson Black to be research.

There were a million different ballet moves and forms that I could teach him, but it dawned on me that unless I knew what he was really struggling with, I wouldn't know where to start. There was no way I would keep his attention if I started from the beginning.

As much as I wanted to treat him as though he was a first time ballerina, fresh into a beginners' class, it felt somewhat wrong. He was an athlete, after all, not to mention an adult. I knew I could spend the coming week going over basics that he would need to know, but then I would be stuck at a crossroads, and would need to have a better idea of what type of things we could work on.

Unfortunately, the news didn't give me much. They showed him dropping two balls, and the rest was just a video of his stupid perfect face while they talked about how awful he was.

I didn't follow sports, but I knew Ty wasn't awful. Mr. Peyton had told me as much. He said something was off, something was getting to him, but that he was one of the best. He was hoping that focusing on something outside of his realm, but also something toward his overall athletic concepts, would help him.

Working with someone like Ty Black really would boost my reputation, but he made it abundantly clear that he didn't want anyone knowing he was learning ballet. He was the type that would give poor Sam a hard time for being a man in what is considered a "girl" sport.

Yes, I considered dancing a sport. It was an activity involving physical exertion and skill. It also involved people competing against one another for entertainment. The only difference was, the competition took place behind the scenes, and the winners were the ones that got to entertain the viewers.

Despite Ty not wanting to let me put his lessons on my website, and the fact that I was kind of using him not to be alone in the studio. Mr. Peyton was offering me enough money to pay the rent on *Brise* for half a year, and that was an offer I couldn't refuse. I had made some money as a dancer, but it was going to run out.

Brise did well as far as a steady clientele. But we had yet to do a performance, and if I didn't get that arranged for the parents, things would start going downhill.

I made a mental note to call a few theaters first thing Monday morning. There were sure to be a few small theaters with something available for November or December. It would be a quick turnaround, but I was confident the kids would be able to put on a show for Christmas.

As far as Sunday went, I was done thinking about the studio and Ty. I needed to take a little time for myself, and I usually did that by working out in the gym of my building. I was on my feet at the studio every day, but nothing beat the hard sweat of weights and cardio.

The gym was in the basement of the building and was always empty on Sundays. A few people would straggle in and out but for the most part, I knew I would have most of the equipment to myself. The isolation added to its appeal for me.

Unfortunately, as I approached the doors, I could hear someone inside very loudly explaining that *they weren't going to put up with that shit anymore.* I sighed out my frustration, but hoped that when I got in there, they would take their conversation elsewhere.

Opening the doors to the state-of-the-art gym, I locked in on the person disturbing my normally silent Sunday.

Mr. Peyton.

Shit, that meant not only would I have to deal with other people, but I would have to be on my 'A' game as well. I couldn't let a man who was paying me to help him see any part of me that didn't exude poise. It was how I worked, how I made my living.

It was all I knew how to be in the face of others.

Pulling my slouched shoulders back, I held my chin up, and I walked by the treadmill that Mr. Peyton was on. He hadn't noticed me yet, so I took a minute to try and figure him out.

He was a nice enough guy from the one time we spoke, but I had seen him on TV, and he was always yelling. According to the sports channels, he had a lot to prove because he was a fairly young coach. Despite winning a few Super Bowls since he arrived in Atlanta, everyone gave the credit to the quarterback, Cam Nichols, and no one gave Mr. Peyton his due respect.

As he continued yelling into the phone, he never missed a beat on his run. You would think he would have trouble yelling while also running, but the fact that he didn't miss a syllable spoke to how in shape he must have been.

He was wearing calf-length joggers and a tight long-sleeved

shirt that accentuated how lithe his body was. I wondered for a minute why he wasn't playing football instead of coaching. Or had he? He looked like he was in better shape than some of the guys I saw on TV. Not Tyson Black, of course.

Ty was in a whole different league. He was almost scary. Exceptionally tall, and his biceps were as round as my thighs.

As I started a small warm-up on the elliptical, I got lost in thought, thinking of Ty's calves, and wondering how they would flex doing an arabesque. It wasn't that I was attracted to him, just that I could appreciate how well he took care of himself as an athlete.

"Ahem." The small noise interrupted my thoughts, and my eyes shot up to see Mr. Peyton standing next to me. I flushed a little knowing I had been thinking of his tight end. Not *his* tight end, but Ty's. No, not Ty's tight end, but his position on the field.

Good God, I was spiraling. Luckily, Mr. Peyton seemed too distracted to notice I had been having an internal battle with myself.

"This is embarrassing," he started to say, "But I forgot your name."

"Um, Giselle," I smiled, slowing down my pace on the elliptical. Unlike Mr. Peyton, I couldn't hold a conversation and workout. As poised and skilled as I was, and as much as I took care of my body, I wasn't risking falling on my face while we chatted.

"Shit of course," he snapped his fingers. "Fancy seeing you here, *Giselle*. Sorry for the yelling, I thought I was alone."

"You were, I just got here. I come in every Sunday. So I should say fancy seeing you here."

"Fair enough," he shrugged as he kept running, taking his gaze back to his screen. "I normally workout at the complex with the players, but they are getting on my damn nerves, so I had to leave for a bit."

"Are you normally there on Sundays when there are no games?"

"Every day," he huffed. "This time of year we're gearing up for the season, and every day is something. There are no days off. Speaking of, how is Ty?"

"Haven't you spoken to him?"

"Of course I have, but he is vague, and gives me more headaches than I can stand."

I laughed because in my two days of seeing Ty, he had already given me a few headaches.

"Ah, you too?" Mr. Peyton smiled. "Trust me, he's arrogant, rough, tough, and I bet he hates me so much for putting him in ballet class like he's a five year old. But he's fucking worth it. If I can figure out what's fucking him up, I'll be the happiest coach alive."

"Well, I will do my best to help," I gave him a *"you're paying me well"* smile and shrugged. "I just wish I could see what it is he needs help with. Any insight there?"

"No clue. Honestly, no clue. I think it's in his head. I was hoping ballet would get him out of his head."

"Yes, but it is so much more. He could learn techniques that match his playing style if I knew what that was. Is there anywhere online that has any good video of him catching and playing? Especially recent ones that could show me his posture?"

Mr. Peyton stopped cocked his head at me, seemingly dumbfounded by what I asked. It was making me feel sheepish for even bringing it up. I may not have wanted to spend a lot of time with Ty Black, but he was a job, and I took all my jobs seriously.

"I have a good idea," he smiled. "Come to practice with me tomorrow."

My eyes widened and I started to shake my head. Poor Mr. Peyton didn't realize I didn't like being around a lot of people. I would be a ball of nerves, and I was 1000% sure Ty would have a coronary if his *ballet teacher* showed up in his big bad tough guy world.

"Um, that is probably not a good idea," I turned my head from side to side trying to think of an obvious and understandable reason why it was so awful.

"It's a great idea. You can stay for an hour and I can have Ty run drills. You can get an idea of his quirks and movements. You are trained in the art of balance and poise. It's why I asked you to do this in the first place. You can probably see things that we can't."

"Mr. Black does not want everyone to know he is taking ballet."

"Oh, trust me, I know all about how much he doesn't want to tarnish his 'bad boy of the league' reputation with his tutu, and I don't really give a fuck. But," he held up a hand so that I would let him finish. "I know his sour attitude would make it harder on you, so we don't have to tell a soul who you are. A lot of teams have professionals come in and observe. You would be treated as such."

I started to turn the idea over in my mind. It really would help me speed things along. Saying yes to Mr. Peyton was an impulse decision when I was scared, but since I had met Ty, it was better that I take the money and run.

Ty was a force against my resolve, and it was only a matter of time before he saw through the frosted glass I built around myself. He drove me nuts, and made it hard to stay in character. Character meaning the persona I kept when I was in the studio.

Ty Black was exhausting.

He was a cross between charming and scary. A teddy bear and a snake. Some part of me knew he was a good guy to have around, and another part of me feared the outcome of having him close for too long. As Mr. Peyton had said, he had a bad boy reputation. It was totally a vibe he exuded, yet he was in control of it when, and where, it presented itself.

"You know what? I think I will take you up on that. Maybe if I can see something, we can get him corrected quicker."

"Great!" he slapped his hands together and turned toward the door. "I have your number from the other night. Why don't I send you directions to the complex, you can follow me if you like."

"Oh, I don't have a car, but I can take the train to the stadium."

"Oh, we don't work out at the stadium during camp, it's out in Johns Creek."

Shit, that was 30 minutes from the center of town.

"I would offer to give you a ride, but I'm there all day and wouldn't be able to bring you back. How about I send a car for you, then they can bring you back to the city after a few hours. Sound good?"

I nodded, accepting that offer. He may have been paying me, but it was definitely a favor in his advantage to get Ty back to form.

"Ok, I'll make sure someone is out front at 9:00 am. Thanks Giselle." He jogged from the room so fast, I giggled. It was like he was sure if he stuck around, I would change my mind.

The next morning, I got dressed for the first time in weeks. No tights, no tutus, no workout clothes, no pajamas. I had on actual slacks that were tailored to my small frame. The blouse was tucked in, my hair was down, and I opted for the blazer that matched the pants.

I may have been overdressed for a football practice, but I wanted to make sure I looked the part that I was asked to fill. A consultant. I wanted to be professional and business-like, and I didn't want to be mistaken for someone that didn't have her shit together.

A sleek black town car drove up to the curb right at nine, and a middle-aged man in a suit hopped out quickly.

"Are you Miss Giselle?" He asked nicely.

"I am," I smiled and put my hand out for him to shake.

He looked confused at first, but returned my firm handshake before motioning to the car.

"Allow me," He opened the door, and I climbed into the soft black interior. When Mr. Peyton said he was sending a car, he sent the best. It reminded me of how my mother preferred to get around New York.

Instead of looking at my phone, I got comfortable and looked out the window to see what was around me. I hadn't had a chance to explore too far outside of the city center, so I was kind of excited to see everything that led to the practice complex.

I'm not sure what I imagined, but even a 30-minute drive didn't take us far from the city. We were still in the thick of traffic when we veered off onto an exit labeled Johns Creek. Maybe I thought there would be land and cows since we were in the heart of the south. Maybe a lake or two?

Don't get me wrong, we were in the suburbs, and there was a lot less mania than downtown. The homes were huge, and the landscapes were perfect. Even the shopping centers were kept up and pristine. I could see the appeal of why people chose to live there when they worked in the busy city.

We drove another mile or so before a wide expanse opened up ahead of us. There was a large gate, and a fence that surrounded the whole place. It looked like a military base, but the sign said, "Welcome to Johns Creek Training Facility. Home of the Atlanta Jets."

The driver rolled his window down, and was waved through without question. He must have done that for the team quite often. He seemed to know exactly where he was headed.

Instead of pulling into a parking spot, or even to the curb, he pulled through another small gate beside a large wall. On the other side was a huge grassy field and two goal posts. On the field the entire Atlanta Jets team was stretching in perfect lines every five yards.

Everything I saw had me in so much awe that it took me a minute to realize the driver had parked and was opening my door, helping me out of the car. I slid my sunglasses on and threw my bag on my shoulder before letting the driver take my hand and lead me safely off the grassy area he parked on.

Standing straight and poised, I started to pull my phone out to call Mr. Peyton and let him know I had arrived, but I heard my name and looked up before hitting send.

"Miss Giselle?"

"Yes," I said to the young guy wearing a Jets polo shirt and khakis.

"I'm Dave, Coach's assistant. He asked me to meet you here and help you out today. Anything you need, I can help you with." He couldn't have been older than 20, which wasn't much younger than I was. Yet, somehow, I felt like a century older than Dave. He was smiling and spry, youthful and energetic.

Those were traits I was capable of, but so rarely got to indulge in. I could picture Dave going to college and drinking on the weekends. He probably had a lot of friends and an exciting social life. I didn't see the Daves of the world much. I only saw ballerina moms, and fellow business associates.

Until Mr. Peyton approached me in the lobby of our building, I hadn't spoken to anyone outside of my professional circle in months. But Mr. Peyton became part of my professional circle, so it didn't even count.

Using some of Dave's energy, I mustered a smile and nodded, letting him know that everything he said was fine by me. I was glad I wasn't going to be left alone. "Lead the way."

CHAPTER SEVEN

"1, 2, 3, 4, 5..."

We were spread out on the lines of the field doing warm-ups before practice. I was with my fellow tight ends on the thirty-yard line, looking into the eyes of the linebackers who were doing the same warm-ups.

It was our dance. We all knew the steps to that dance, and performed as a coordinated unit. The choreography was the same every morning, and we synchronized ourselves so that if someone was looking on from afar, they would think it was rehearsed.

It was kind of therapeutic in a way. Warm-ups were the only thing during our day that we could predict. No one got hurt, no punches were thrown, no coaches were yelling, and the heat of the day had yet to peak.

Closing my eyes, I took a deep breath as we started our count again and moved on to the next stretch. I was doing my 7th lunge when Duncan Rhodes, one of our backup linebackers, interrupted the count.

"Daaaaaamn, girl," I opened my eyes to see he was staring off to the side of the field. "The honey that just stepped out of the car. Who the fuck is that?"

The few of us who heard him turned our heads and looked at a woman standing next to a town car. Dave was jogging toward her, waving his arms to get her attention. Lucky Dave.

Duncan was right, *Daaaamn.* Only she was not a girl, she was a fucking woman. From where I was, I couldn't see her very well, but that suit made me feel things. Just like when I saw Miss Priss in her tutu, my cock was stirring below my belt.

Who knew I would have a sudden penchant for women *in* clothes? I was usually the kind of guy that found them sexier out of their clothes. But as it turned out, I was into a power suit, because I got lured in just enough to get out of sync with the rest of the team.

"Black," one of the coaches yelled. "Get back in step."

I did without any issues, but I kept my eyes turned toward the woman talking to Dave. He was waving his arms around as if he was Vanna White showing the prize pack for the night. I was curious about who would wear that suit out here, and give a shit about the goings on of camp. So much so that Dave was assigned to her side.

Not that Dave was a big wig, but he was Coach's right-hand man, and Coach didn't do well without him being at his beck and call. So what was so important? Who was so important?

I took my eyes off the woman and got back into a full-force motion for my warm-up. The last thing I needed to do was have something, or someone else, distracting me from football. The media showed up to our afternoon scrimmages, and I needed to make sure I was on my game that morning so I didn't have to deal with their bullshit later.

Warmups, position drills, and touch-and-go's were all I needed to worry about until our scrimmage, so I closed my eyes again, trying to repeat that in my head, trying to focus and visualize. Not sure if that would work but some guys did it, and it beat the shit out of ballet lessons with Miss Priss. If I could get it right, I could talk Coach into quitting my extracurricular activities.

"Stop." Whistles blew and Coach's voice came in from the sideline. He was waving his arms, and all the coaches were mimicking him to get us to gather around. Not only did he interrupt our dance, but he was interrupting our routine.

The new woman was standing beside him, her sunglasses on and her long dark hair was wavy around her shoulders. Her face was grim, and for a second, I thought maybe someone died, and she was the person sent to dismantle the team.

I got as close as I could, but considering there were a hundred of us in camp, it was quite a crowd. The guys in the front started to kneel, and when the ones right in front of me knelt, I had the perfect view.

"Guys. We are gonna do things a little differently this morning. Instead of touch-and-go drills, I want you in position drills for the next hour. However, I want the tight ends with the quarterbacks."

The fuck?

I looked over to our quarterback, Cam Nichols, who was standing on the edge of the group. He looked just as confused as I was, so whatever was up Coach's sleeve was news to us all.

"I want to introduce you to Giselle Metrovik," Coach started. My eyes shot wide and I looked back at the woman. There was no way that was Giselle. Not *my* Giselle. Not Miss Priss. Not Miss Sprints Through the Park at ten pm every night.

Wait, my Giselle?

She took off her sunglasses, and those eyes looked around the group of players as she gave a tight smile, and waited for Coach to keep talking.

"She's a special consultant and will be here for a few hours. She'll be taking a look at you all, and trying to figure out where you are lacking."

I snorted and shook my head, catching the attention of everyone, including Giselle and Coach.

"Problem, Black?" Coach asked, daring me to speak up.

He knew what the fucking problem was, and I knew I should have been thankful he referred to her as a consultant and not my ballet teacher. But it was still fucked up.

"Nope," I popped and put my hands on my hips. Coach kept his eyes on me, silently putting me on the spot, but I wasn't going to give him the satisfaction of seeing me uncomfortable. Besides, maybe he wanted her there to watch the other guys. Maybe he wanted me to have classmates in my ballet lessons. A group lesson.

"Okay then, Nichols, Black, you two head to field 3." I looked over to Cam, who shrugged and started walking. All of our morning practices were non-contact, so there was no need for pads and helmets. We wore shorts and our jerseys. So when Coach said go to field three, I had nothing else to grab, or do, but start walking behind Cam.

"What the fuck is going on?" I asked Cam from behind, but he just shrugged again and kept walking.

Easy for him to do. He wasn't struggling. Cam was kicking ass like he always did. No one ever got on his case about how shitty his playing was, so he didn't have a care in the damn world.

I looked back and saw the rest of the guys being distributed into groups between the four fields we had here at the training complex. It was no surprise that Dave was escorting Giselle to field three.

"Heads up," Cam yelled and a ball flew my way. I caught it and threw it back, helping him warm his arm up while we waited on the coaches—and apparently Miss Priss—to join us.

Lawrence Anders, another tight end, jogged up and started throwing with us while watching Giselle and Coach walk our way. He didn't say anything, but he was thinking what the rest of the guys were thinking. That the new consultant was unbelievably gorgeous.

Shit, even as uptight as she was, there was no denying Giselle's appeal. Add her long dark waves being out of her normal bun, the power suit, and sunglasses, and I was surprised she didn't have a line of guys following her like baby ducks.

Something about the thought of them giving her any attention didn't sit right with me, though. Giselle wasn't mine, even though I had just referred to her as such, nor would she ever be.

Nor did I want her to be.

But I felt some sort of claim over her because I saw her first. She was my dance instructor, and even though I would rather die than let these guys know I was taking ballet, I didn't want them to give her any nods either.

So I shouldn't have been surprised when I found myself next to Lawrence, who still had his tongue hanging out, and pushed him hard enough he almost fell to the ground.

"What the fuck?" He yelled, and had Cam running to get in between us.

"Pay attention," I deflected.

"I was, you motherfucker."

"Hey, hey hey…" Cam was trying to intervene and keep us separated.

"No, you had your eyes over there," I nodded toward Coach and Giselle. Coach was now running to us, leaving Giselle to walk slowly with Dave.

"What's it to you?" Lawrence yelled louder, getting angrier.

"It matters because we needed your head over here," I shot hands between Cam and me, indicating Lawrence should have been focusing on us.

"Are you fucking ki—"

"Hey," Coach yelled as he approached. "What the hell is happening over here?"

Lawrence backed up since Coach was there and jutted his

chin at me. "Black's pushing people like we're on the playground, Coach. Telling me to focus on a game of catch. Pretty big coming from the same motherfucker that can't catch a pass to save his damn life."

"Oh, you wanna go there?" I started charging Lawrence again, but Coach put himself in between us as Cam grabbed Lawrence from behind. His arms were around his shoulders and he was saying something to him to calm him down.

'Enough!" Coach yelled, throwing his hat on the ground. "We aren't starting our day off going at each other. Get your shit together now. Or I'll send you home."

No one wanted to go home. We were in camp. No one went home during camp. Most of the guys didn't leave the complex for anything. No one knew that I was leaving at eight every night and coming back at ten-thirty. By then, most of the guys were passed out from a hard day's practice and they all thought I was one of them.

Instead, Coach had me driving my ass into the city for ballet lessons. Thinking about that made me realize that was why I was frustrated. It wasn't that he was looking at Giselle, it was that I was so fucking tired. I didn't get the rest that the others got. I hadn't earned that right by having a good practice. While they were all eating and sleeping like babies at the end of the day, I was doing ballet.

Rage burned in my ears as I slowly realized that all I really needed was a fucking nap. I backed off of Lawrence and threw my hands up. It wasn't his fault I was in the position I was in, and shoving a teammate wasn't exactly setting myself up for a good day.

However, when Giselle approached, and Lawrence smiled his smarmy lips at her, nodding and raising his brows, I started to lunge at him again. It was like I couldn't even stop myself.

Thankfully, Cam was standing next to me and grabbed my

arm, realizing what I was about to do. "Get down the field, Black, the ball is headed your way."

Cam grabbed a football off the grass and tapped it, showing me he was about to air one down the field. I looked to Coach, and then Giselle, who was watching me intently, waiting to see what I did.

I started running, ready to show them all that I could catch anything, anytime, anywhere. But when Cam called a signal, one that told me I needed to stop on the 40-yard line and turn to my right, I got my feet wrapped up, and ended up with a ball ricocheting against my right shoulder.

"Damnit," I yelled, wanting to blame the mistake on my laces or something while also rubbing the sting in my shoulder.

"Black," Coach yelled. "I want you taking passes from Nichols nonstop."

I shook my head, but only at myself. Getting passes from our number one quarterback wasn't a bad deal, but knowing it was because I had fucked up stung worse than my shoulder.

Jogging back down to stand beside Cam, I waited while the other quarterbacks and tight ends teamed up for passes of their own. Giselle was standing at the 50-yard line, her hands on her hips and her head looking at everyone but me. It made me feel better that she was watching everyone, but I still wanted to talk to Coach.

"Coach, can I talk to you?" I waved him over and gave Cam a look that asked for some privacy. Cam, being the classy guy he was, didn't even bat an eye and walked away as Coach approached.

"What's up, Black?"

"What's she doing here?"

"I told you she is consulting," he snapped back.

"I don't want her here." Even I could tell I sounded like a fucking baby, and I cringed at my own words.

"Well, that isn't up to you. The only reason I haven't already sent you to the showers this morning is so she can watch you work for a bit. The only reason I'm even entertaining this conversation is because I know asking you to do ballet was a little messed up. But I do what I want, and what is best for the team, not what is best for Tyson Black. So you can suck it up and play catch with Nichols, or you can sit on the bench for our first preseason game in two weeks."

With that, he turned around and casually walked off. I was an idiot for even bringing it up because he was right, he called the shots. If I wanted to play, I would play by his rules. And because my game sucked, I didn't have much room to complain.

Biting my lip to keep from screaming, I looked back to Giselle who was tapping on an iPad that she most likely pulled out of the bag she carried. She was asking Dave a few questions and he was pointing to people that weren't me.

After a minute, she must have sensed me staring because she turned her head and looked directly at me. There was no one else she could have been looking at so I held her gaze, squinting a little to show my anger, and waited for her to get intimidated and look away.

She didn't.

She held my eyes while resting the iPad on her hip and cocked her head to one side. It was a taunt, and she added to its effect when she lifted one side of her mouth in a half smile. Miss Priss knew her presence was getting to me, and she was somehow finding enjoyment from it. I hadn't seen her like that before.

Granted, I didn't know her well enough to assume she was always so cold, but she was fucking frigid when we were in her studio. That power suit must have been doing more for her than it was for me.

Still biting my lip, I gave her a wink, doing a little taunting of my own. Then I slid my tongue out over my bottom lip and across my teeth, causing her to look a little flushed, but she didn't turn her head. Not until Cam called me, and interrupted our little dance, did I turn away. I gave my quarterback and team captain my attention and respect.

"Go long," he said with a smirk. I didn't allow myself to dwell on whether he noticed something between Giselle and me. He'd never guess the connection if he tried. So I just took off in a sprint and listened for him to make a call.

When he yelled the play, I knew I needed to go left and turn at the 30-yard line, so I did and thanked the heavens above that the ball flew right into my gut with an easy catch. You'd have thought I had just put the eight ball in the corner pocket though, with the way I swaggered back to Cam, gently tossing him the ball.

Giselle had her head back in her iPad when I peeked over, but I imagined her taking notes on me: "*Superb catch. He is a master of his craft, and quite capable of returning to his star form without my help.*"

giselle

NO BALANCE ON TAKE-OFF. *No visual focus tells. No poise after the catch.*

My list of things Ty was doing wrong was long, but so were the other notes I had taken. Some of the other guys were struggling as well and I couldn't help myself. Honestly, it seemed like there was a lack of communication, but that didn't make sense because their coaches were right there. They could hear and see everything, so who was I to assume that was the problem.

I decided to concentrate on what I did know—balance, posture, strength, coordination, and flexibility. I jotted notes until I had to excuse myself to get back into the city to open the studio for classes.

Mondays were fairly easy because I didn't have to stay late with the advanced kids. I was home before dark, and enjoyed a nice bath and comfort food. Some people hated Mondays but I cherished them.

Once I had opened the studio, I was warming up my legs, waiting on my beginners to start trickling in, when two police officers walked into the reception room. Through the large window, I saw them asking my receptionist something before they all looked my way.

I swallowed down my nerves and initial concern, making my way to the door to greet them.

"Hi, officers, may I help you?" I asked in my normal professional tone.

"Yes ma'am, you are Giselle Metrovik, correct?"

I nodded, "That is correct."

"We are just here to follow up on the incident that happened the other night. Is there anywhere we can talk?" He looked back where one of my littlest dancers had come in with her mom and was getting her proper shoes on by the cubbies.

"Of course," I motioned toward the back room where I had an office I rarely used. I led them in, and they shut the door before standing in front of my desk while I shifted behind it, staying on my feet with my shoulders pushed back.

"Ok," one of the officers got right to it. "We just wanted to follow up and check in, first of all."

"What happened to the officers on the case? That showed up the other night?"

"Those were street cops, but this case has been moved to the CIU. More specifically, the gang unit."

"Gang?"

"Yes, ma'am, we believe we have discovered a connection between what happened here, and a few other businesses that week. There is also a connection to gang activity so we don't think that what you experienced was a fluke, or random."

"What does that even mean?" I felt my poise slipping. It was a good neighborhood. An upscale part of town that rarely saw gang activity. I had decided that what happened was a robbery, one that didn't take place because he realized once he was in that I only had tutus and tap shoes. When the coast was clear, he bailed and tried elsewhere.

Why couldn't that really be the story?

"It means that your business may have been marked as a 'zone' for gang members roaming the streets. If they need a place to hide while the cops, or their rivals go by, this might be where they run to."

"Are you saying it could happen again?" I completely lost my composure and was shaking. Fear was seeping through my veins.

"We're saying we need you to be vigilant, and keep your doors locked at all times. Until we can find out who is playing on this side of town and put a stop to it, we have no patterns or tells that can lead us to an arrest right now."

Falling back into my chair, I blew out a loud breath. It sounded like something that would take a lot longer than a couple of weeks to solve. I had talked myself into it being a one-time thing, and that I would start feeling safe again soon.

I also knew that having Ty around on Tuesdays and Thursdays was pointless. What good was he in a gang fight? What good would having someone there with me be when that extra presence wouldn't be enough to deter the one who wanted in?

They wouldn't go another way because there was a man in there with me. They would rather hide from the law, from other gangs, from things that were far worse than a tatted-up football player with a bad attitude.

Somehow, I thanked the officers for stopping by, and for the information, even though I felt zoned out. Despite their warning, I didn't lock the doors, because how could I? I had moms and dads with their little dancers coming in and out all day. But I managed to make it through the afternoon classes with no incident, and locked the studio up without having a panic attack.

If I told everyone what was happening, worry would ensue. But was I putting kids in danger by not being honest? Was staying open the right thing to do?

Shutting a business down completely was asinine, and not feasible. Especially one like mine that needed to stay open for financial reasons alone. I wanted to see what the other businesses did, to see if they were as fearful as I was. The officers said they would email me a list of the ones they thought were marked, so maybe I should wait until I saw that list. I wanted to know I was not the only one cutting and running at the fear of a recurring incident.

I mulled over what was right, and what was wrong, all the way home. I was less fearful during the daylight hours on a crowded sidewalk and park. Especially once I knew it was not me that was the target, but my business.

Once inside my apartment, I didn't relax like I normally did. There was no extravagant meal, or a hot bath. I went straight to my couch and pulled up my notes from the Jets' practice that morning. I had also used the camera on my iPad to take some video and wanted to see what I had for footage.

I hoped focusing on that for a while would ease my worries. Plus, I wanted to send Mr. Peyton some notes sooner rather than later.

I pulled up a video that I knew was of Ty and pressed play. I didn't know what the timing of their plays were, so I had started recording way before the quarterback actually threw the ball. That meant the first few minutes was nothing but footage of Ty standing there, talking to the quarterback, and shaking his hands and feet to stay loose.

One part of me wanted to fast forward to the play, another part of me left my finger hovering over the scroll button, and never actually doing anything. Ty Black may have been struggling, but he didn't look the part. He had a swagger that appealed to me. Confidence, even in his time of defeat.

When he tilted his neck, I could see the veins popping and the tattoos moving. He was tight, even when he was loose. For practice, he had worn shorts and a jersey with his number on it—82. The jersey hugged right above his waistline and I could see the definition of his ass from behind.

He had run a play before I realized I was focusing on all the wrong parts of the video. All I had mentally taken note of was the fact that he was not wearing a cup as he jogged and moved toward the direction of the camera.

With that realization, I threw my iPad over to the side of my couch and stood up. What the hell was wrong with me? My brain was all over the place. One second, I was worried and scared. The next, I was lusting over a hot football player.

What I really needed to do was let loose for a bit. It had been way too long since I let my hair down and had some fun. I had been so worried about failing in Atlanta, that I had not let myself be anyone except the studious ballet instructor with a prodigious background.

I had to get through the week, but I decided by Friday I would take myself somewhere. I would do something. The thought of having the relief was enough to make me grab my iPad and start looking over videos again.

Only this time, I steer clear of Ty Black videos. I knew he was the one I was supposed to be helping, but he had already figured out how studious I was, and it seemed like he made it his mission to make me crack. Even when he wasn't trying to.

Even when he didn't know he was doing it.

CHAPTER NINE

WE WERE in our last week of camp and I was fucking exhausted. Too tired to barely lift my legs, yet somehow I was expected to do ballet again.

Coach told me Miss Priss hadn't gotten back to him on anything from her time at practice, at least not on me. He had received several notes on Lawrence, though.

Not sure if that made me mad, or vindicated. When I asked Coach if she was there to watch Lawrence, he told me the truth. She was there to watch me, but if she saw anything she could help with, she would send the info his way.

"I may see if Lawrence wants to go with you on Tuesday and Thursday to work out whatever she's got for you," Coach had said.

No way was I going to have a witness to my efforts in the degrading "sport" of ballet. I didn't care if Lawrence would also be subjected, we weren't going to be skipping into that place like two little girls ready for class.

"You sure that's the reason?" Coach smirked.

"Fuck yeah," I scoffed while turning and leaving his office. I didn't believe me, though, so I doubt he believed me either. I had been with Giselle three times if you included the practice, and every time had been somewhat fun. Getting her riled up and seeing how she responded was something I was looking forward to, and I sure as fuck didn't want Lawrence involved.

At exactly 9:00 pm the next night, I tried opening the door to the studio, but it was locked. Peeking through the slit in the blinds was hard, but I had just sat there and watched the munchkins leave, so I knew she was in there.

"Hey, Miss Priss," I knocked and yelled.

It only took a minute, and she was unlocking the door and ushering me in quickly.

"Come in, come in," she whispered.

She locked the door again once we were inside and peeked through the blinds. While I waited on her, I took my shoes off and set my keys on a chair inside the lobby. The noise they made against the plastic of the chair made Giselle twirl around. She was anxious, but gave me her best fake smile.

"Hi, so good to see you. Time to get started." The worry lines still lingered in her features, but she clapped twice, and I knew that was my cue to get started.

Walking behind her from the reception area to the studio, I paid close attention to her body language. Her shoulders had tension, and her steps were short. Her neck barely moved, and her fists were clenching and unclenching.

"You ok?" I was genuinely concerned, even though I knew it wasn't my place to care.

"Of course." She turned and had the same fake smile on her face.

I chewed my lip and nodded, letting it go because I wasn't anyone to her. I didn't want to push. Plus, I had an asshole reputation to uphold, and I needed to get to work on that.

"Good, because I came up with some things that you suck at."

"Excuse me?"

"You're too thin, for one." I held up one finger and ticked it off with the fingers on my other hand. "Second of all, I am 87% sure you have a stick shoved way up your ass."

She started to turn red, and I could see her slipping from the poise she tried carrying. Normally, that poise was infallible, but I could sense tonight she was weak, and I pounced.

"Also," I ticked a third finger. "You don't belong on a football field. You looked ridiculous." Fuck that was a lie. She looked like she was there to do a job, and like we should have all been bowing down to her superiority. But I was on a roll, and her face was telling me I was hitting the right buttons.

"That we can agree on, Mr. Black," she spoke through clenched teeth. "I did not want to be near that field, but when I ran into Mr. Peyton in the gym of our building, we came up with a plan to expedite your ballet lessons to help you improve on the field."

"Did it work?"

"I do not know yet, instead of discussing that, you have been insulting me."

"Whatever." I shook my head and smiled incredulously, feeling like I finally had the upper hand. I started to turn away, feeling like I could mic drop and strut.

"Did you notice you are stepping off from your heels when you run?"

I swung my head back to her and squinted in disbelief. "I've played football my whole life, and I just now forgot how to run?"

"Maybe? Or maybe you are not thinking about it, so your body is making the motion without your consent."

"What the fuck?"

"We need to retrain you to push off with your toes." She grabbed the case of the iPad she had at practice the day before and walked toward me. "Let me show you what I mean."

She got close to me, closer than she had been before. Close enough that, for the first time, I could smell her, and feel her. She smelled floral, and her arm against mine felt warm and soft. The top of her bun came to my shoulders, and from standing right behind her left shoulder, I could see her iPad clearly.

She hit play, and I saw myself setting up on the line, waiting for Cam to say go. She played it once at regular speed, and slowed it down the second time. The video zoomed in on my feet and she was not fucking wrong, I was flat-footed and didn't even realize it.

If I had thought that video was a fluke, she continued to show me several more with the same problem. Over and over again, I took off slowly from my heel, like she had said. She left the iPad in my hands and walked away, but I kept hitting replay.

"Fuck!" I yelled before throwing her iPad across the room. "What else, Miss Perfect?"

She jumped at my outburst, and her eyes started darting side to side. I scared the fuck out of her, and didn't mean to, but seeing myself fuck up in the most basic manner was a hard pill to swallow.

"Sorry," I muttered, picking the iPad up from the floor. It wasn't broken, so I closed the case and handed it to her. She gently took it and set it on the table she had by the mirror.

"Um," she started, which caught my attention. She never said words like 'um.' She was too put together for the likes of such a mundane word. "Let's try to focus a little. In ballet, we learn the classical walk early on. That would have been a few weeks away for us, but since I was able to see its need firsthand, we can head straight to it."

I tamped down my anger, and took my spot facing the mirror. She stood a few feet away and encouraged me to follow along with her movements. "When a dancer walks, they are rolling through their foot starting with the toe, into the ball of the foot, then finally the heel. Also, the dancer must keep their legs and feet turned right the whole time."

She did a walk and then motioned for me to mimic her. I was too pissed at myself to argue, so I followed her instruction and made changes when she told me to. We walked from one side of the studio to the other, and after a while, her excitement started shining through.

"Yes!" she clapped once. "You have it."

I felt like an idiot, prancing around the fucking wooden floor and pointing my toes. But I had to admit, her excitement was worth my pain. It was almost infectious, and had I not been a little rough around the edges, I would have clapped, too.

"Now, let's go across one more time, but this time, I want you to close your eyes and focus. I want you to tune everything out and see in your mind the way your feet are touching."

"Wouldn't it make more sense if I did this on the field instead of here?" I mean, shit, didn't it?

She shrugged, which was another un-Miss Priss-like move. "It is not uncommon for football players to take ballet. I think they just keep it to themselves. But this is an environment where there are no other jobs. All you have to do here is focus on pointed toes. Or focus on whatever we need to. The field is loud for a player, and this is an alternative place to find those steps."

That actually made sense, and I wondered who else on my team had taken ballet and I didn't know about it. Coach was the one that set it up, so I wondered if he ever had. It didn't make it any less awkward, but I was curious if I could apply it on the field the next day.

"So that's it? We're done?"

"You and I both wish, Mr. Black. Thursday, we need to talk about twirling your body more fluidly."

I didn't respond, just closed my eyes and started classical walking across the studio. When I got close to the other wall, I opened my eyes and turned a little twirl, hoping I could show Giselle that I was a master twirler already, making me almost fall.

But that almost-fall created a miracle.

Giselle laughed. A real and full laugh that showed teeth and tongue and tears. She put a hand on her hip and shook her head.

"Yep, working on that Thursday," was all she said before gathering her things.

I smirked at her, somehow lighter since I knew she was capable of laughing. Not to mention, I had heard more than one contraction in her vocabulary, and I'd never forget her use of the word "Um." She was almost likable, and it made me smile as I made my way to the door of the studio and slid my shoes on.

She was already waiting by the door to let us out, and maybe it was the lighter spirit, or maybe it was just my curiosity, but I had to ask. "You walk home in that?"

She looked down at herself and swiped a hand down her skirt. "Only on Tuesdays and Thursdays since I'm here late. Saves time not to change."

"I can wait on you if you want to change," I suggested, wondering if she was scared to be alone. From the way she reacted and ran across the park, she was clearly scared of something.

"Another insult?" she asked, tilting her head.

"No, just offering," I shrugged. "Didn't know if you preferred to cover up before walking home."

"How do you know I walk?"

My eyes widened because I didn't want to tell her I watched her actually run, but I quickly thought of an excuse. "You and Coach live in the same building, and it's across the park, so I just assumed."

"I am fine." She spoke quickly, trying to get herself back to her uptight ways.

"Sure thing." I held my hands up in surrender. But I was aggravated, probably more than I should have been. Her tights and her short skirt may have covered her skin, but it didn't leave much to the imagination. If something, or someone, spooked her, walking around like that was not a good idea.

We walked out of the front door, and I hung around as she locked up. I could see her hands starting to shake, and she was having trouble getting the key into the hole. I pretended not to notice because she prided herself on her poise, but more than before, I saw it slipping, and it was killing me.

When I first met her, I thought it would be fun to see her break, but only if I was the one who broke her. I didn't like the fact that she was shaken up by something, or someone else.

After she got the lock turned, she started walking across the street and toward the sidewalk next to the park. I could tell she wanted to start running, but she wouldn't as long as I was in sight. Instead of veering down the alley toward my car, I got beside her and walked.

"What are you doing?" she asked but didn't stop.

"Gotta go see Coach," I lied.

I walked into *Brise*, ready to bring her down a notch the way she had done to me, but I was left feeling a tad protective and worried. I knew she wouldn't let me walk her home without an excuse, though.

Coach was at the complex. He only went home on the weekends, if that, but Giselle didn't need to know that I felt better about seeing that she got home okay.

I could have settled on watching her like I had the week before, but I wanted her to feel safe. I may not have liked being in ballet. I may not even have liked Miss Priss that much. But I wasn't a complete jerk, and in a matter of an hour, she had grown on me a bit.

She didn't acknowledge what I said, just let me keep walking beside her. When we got to the lobby, I faked an incoming phone call and told her I would see her Thursday. My fake phone call was one that I had to take before I went up.

Once the elevator closed her in, I walked back to my car, and with a few steps left, I lifted my head and arms, doing a classical walk alone in the alley.

I was fucked.

giselle

"MISS METRO!" Alycia jumped into the studio with excitement on her face.

"Yes?" I folded my hands together like a prayer and tilted my chin up. I tried to be professional with the kids, but I also understood their different level of understanding than adults. Kids just wanted someone kind, and happy to see them.

"My mom said we're going to do a dance for lots of people," she was jumping in place, the excitement never waning. I looked up to see her mom walking to a chair behind the window, and she smiled at me, clearly pleased I had finally arranged a small production.

"We are," I replied, happy to see my efforts being rewarded with enthusiasm.

All week, I called every small theater I could and, by Wednesday, had almost given up. Luckily, there was a theater in Buckhead, aptly called The Buckhead Theater, that had an opening on the first Thursday in December due to a canceled show.

That canceled show was an intimate concert by a world-famous country duo. Agreeing to let our little ballet company fill that void for the low cost of what we could afford was harder than it should have been. They knew we couldn't charge parents more than a nominal fee, and they also knew we wouldn't fill up their 1800 seating capacity. So I promised a celebrity surprise guest and may have mentioned my mother's name.

It wasn't a proud moment for me, and I would have to beg her to come appear in our show, but it got the job done. But on December 2nd, *Brise's* advanced ballet and tap classes would be performing a small Christmas collection for family and friends.

Once it was confirmed, I sent an email to all the parents, and based on the smiles of not only Alycia's mom, but all the others, they were happy—maybe even impressed. They didn't know I had let it slip and didn't have it planned months ago, and I wasn't going to tell them because I needed a win.

While I let myself focus on securing the show, I almost forgot about the probability of gangs infiltrating our little part of town and using the studio as a home base. That may have been an exaggeration, but I didn't know anything about gang life, and was scared.

With the recital all set, I had no choice but to push through and keep *Brise* open. I called the officers who came by and asked if the kids were in danger. He eased my worries by telling me they most likely knew the place was unlocked and empty after dark, and that was why I had been targeted. *"Even bad guys didn't want to mess with kids."*

They assured me the business was fine unless I was alone after dark. Even though I learned to lock the door, a shiver still ran down my spine when I thought about it. Ty came on those late nights, but for how long? Not that he could do anything to help. If anything, I was just putting him in danger without telling him.

As the kids finished filing in, I got them in their places with a quick clap and looked around at their little faces. They had all been informed about the show by their parents, but it was my turn to explain the importance of the next few months.

"Class, as you may have…" I stopped talking when I realized the X in the back of the room was empty.

Sam. That was Sam's spot, and he wasn't there. He never missed a class, and he was never late, so I was immediately worried.

The class noticed where my eyes had stopped, and the older kids started giggling. "I wonder if Sam found a boy sport to play?"

"Enough," I cut their remarks off before they could continue. I taught ballet because it was what I knew how to do, and I thrived when I saw talent like Sam's, but one of the reasons I left the stage was because of girls like the ones laughing in front of me. Even if for a different reason, it was still a hard pill to swallow when I realized that mean girls started young, and I would still be surrounded by them even away from the big stage.

Brise needed to be better than that. I had to set a better example. The students needed to know bullying would not be tolerated in my studio.

Gathering my thoughts, I waited a few more minutes before I tried to continue.

"As I was saying, your parents may have told you about the performance we will be doing the first weekend of December at The Buckhead Theater. It is not the Fox Theater in terms of size, but it is famous for having big acts and a grand stage. We will be the first ballet company to perform on their stage, and I hope you realize the honor you will have to be a part of this show. We will need to work hard, and show up to every class. Sometimes, you may even be asked to practice at home, and more than likely, we will have extra classes on the weekends as the show gets closer."

A hand shot up in the middle row, and I turned my attention to the tiny dancer. "Yes, Madeline?"

"Can we do a Christmas dance?"

"We will do the whole show with a Christmas theme. It will be an exciting start to the holiday season."

The girls started jumping and giggling, talking amongst themselves. I let them get their excitement out for a moment while I looked at Sam's empty X one more time. I wanted Sam to dance the lead. I couldn't wait to tell him, and it was killing me that he was missing class.

"Ok, time to start," I clapped twice, and just like they were taught to do, they silenced and got into *en face*. The news of the show had everyone ready to begin. I just hoped that momentum carried them through December.

We went over the songs I had chosen for the set and started with the basics of the routine. We were going to do several songs to tell the story of Christmas, and not all of the kids would be in every dance. That would make it easier for them to learn fewer numbers, but harder for me to separate the teaching process.

With only fifteen minutes left in class, I was facing the window of my parents when I saw the front door open on the side of the reception area.

Instinctually, I screamed, convinced someone was coming in again with a gun and an inclination to hit me with it again.

Or worse, shoot it at the kids.

I started to tell the kids to get down, when Sam's little face peeked around the open door, followed by his mother, Mrs. Warson, and a taller boy behind her—his brother, I assumed. The other parents had noticed my fear, heard my scream, and were already standing in front of their chairs, trying to decide what to do.

I shook my head and silently apologized, laughing at myself, and waving off the adrenaline I still had coursing through me.

My laugh was fake.

My wave was fake.

Everything was fake.

I was thankful it was Sam, but I was worried I would never stop living in fear. Atlanta wasn't supposed to be a place I feared.

It was my freedom, my new path, my new life. I was angry that one scary night changed it all.

Sam opened the doors to the studio and walked in, taking his position on his X. He looked sad, mad, and maybe even embarrassed. His mom was standing by the window with her arms folded, eyeing her son to make sure he was doing as he was supposed to. The other boy had found a chair in the back to slouch down in, uninterested.

I took a moment to welcome him to class, and we continued with the steps I was teaching. The best part about Sam was that he was a natural, and dancing came easily to him, so I knew he would catch up in no time.

By the time class ended, he was already in step with everyone, and seemed to be in a better mood. It was like dancing was the therapy he needed for whatever had him upset in the first place. It used to be the same for me, and it was a look that I recognized. I just didn't know what had caused him to be down in the first place, and I wasn't sure if it was my place to ask, or be concerned.

Thankfully, I didn't have to war with myself too long because when everyone else left, Sam walked to the front of the studio as his mom looked on from the other room.

"Hi, Miss Metro," Sam whispered sheepishly.

"Hi, Sam." I was patient and waited for whatever he needed to say.

"Sorry, I was late," he mumbled with his head down, chin against his chest. "I, um..." he lifted his head and looked back toward the window. His mom had lifted an eyebrow at him, urging him to keep talking. It became apparent at that moment that whatever the cause of his tardiness, his mom did not approve. She was tough, and I was pretty sure poor Sam was in trouble.

"Why were you late?" I brought his attention back to me. knowing I needed to be stern, I strengthened my tone a little.

"I, um...." he looked back one more time at his mom, and her hands went from crossed over her chest to on her hips. Poor Sam had better start talking. I was almost worried about what he was going to say. Did he get in a fight? Bad grades?

"I didn't want to come," he said quietly.

"You didn't want to come?" Sam loved to dance. He always wanted to be there, so my first instinct was disbelief. "Why not?"

Sam shrugged and I looked up to his mom again, that time a worried look in my eye. She nodded at me to make Sam keep talking. For being only eleven years old, Sam was tall, and I barely had to crouch to look him in the eye. But I did so that I could force him to tell me what was really going on.

"Someone at school found out I did ballet and now I'm the joke of the whole school. I want to quit, but my mom won't let me."

Oh Sam.

My heart was breaking into a million pieces, and instead of keeping myself poised, I let go and sank to my knees, taking Sam with me on the way down. It was all I could do to not cry for him.

He sat in front of me, and I hugged him, rocking side to side, hoping I could give him the strength to do what he loved no matter what anyone else said. Kids were so cruel, and the ones who never learned not to be cruel ended up being cruel adults. It made me angry and scared. I wanted to fight for Sam, and every other kid that was bullied for being their true selves.

"Sam, I am so sorry you had to experience a bully for doing something you love. Middle school is hard enough, but when you have kids that make it harder, I can actually understand why you want to quit."

"You do? You won't be mad at me?"

"Not at all. Not only will I not be mad at you, but I will also not let you quit." If he thought I would just nod and bid him farewell, he thought wrong. I was going to fight for him and encourage him to keep going. In the end, if I tried my hardest and he still wanted to walk away, I would let him, but I needed to try to help him first.

"I don't want to come here anymore, Miss Metro. I want to try playing football like the other guys."

At the mention of football, I cringed a little. Tyson Black popped into my mind. Ty was built for a physical sport. When he was Sam's age, I imagined him being twice Sam's size.

Sam's legs were built for flying and jeté-ing his way to a stage. But how did I tell him that? I didn't want to break his spirit, no matter how much I thought football was the wrong choice.

"What does your mom say?"

"She said I had to finish this month because it was paid for by a scholarship, but I don't want you to give me a place in the show because I'm leaving."

"Sam, you are the best dancer I have. I want you on the center of that stage in December being everything you can be. I know being different is hard, but it makes us strong. You can be stronger than those bullies by not letting them win."

Tears started running down Sam's face, and I instinctually went back to hugging him. I was rocking him back and forth like a baby, wondering if it was doing the opposite of making him strong, and still not being able to stop.

Once I felt Sam was okay, I backed away and looked into his eyes. "I will let this conversation end for the night. I have a month to remind you why you should be here, and I plan on doing just that."

Sam nodded with a sad smile, unconvinced by my words. We both started to stand and I looked down to brush off my knees— even though the floor was spotless. I had barely looked up when I heard Sam gasp and squeal.

"That's Tyson Black!" Sam yelled.

Looking through the window, I saw Ty leaning on the wall behind Sam's mom, his arms and legs crossed, watching me.

I had been so consumed with Sam that I almost forgot Ty was

coming. One glance at the clock and I realized it was 9:05. Ty had probably been there for five minutes watching me have a meltdown with Sam. What was more concerning than that, though, was the fact that Sam had just proclaimed his desire to want to play football and there Ty was in all his football glory.

Was it wrong to hope Ty recognized Sam's legs as a strong dancer and suggest Sam stayed away from football? Was I being selfish? Was I overreacting because of my own experiences?

All I really knew was that Sam was running toward the door, and Ty was about to be bombarded by one excited little boy. I hoped that no matter what he said to him, he was good to Sam. I was about to find out a lot about Ty Black.

As Sam ran from the door, Ty stood straight and let his arms hang. A smile passed across his face, and he held a hand up for Sam to give him a high-five. Sam didn't miss a beat, and he jumped up to reach Ty's hand. I couldn't hear what they were saying, and I didn't think I wanted to, but I inched closer to the door anyway.

"You're my favorite player ever," Sam was saying to Ty, who was casually leaning on the chair in front of him, making his arms flex.

"Thanks, man," Ty smiled. "Hoping we have a good season this year."

"Me too, but you're gonna have to have to catch the ball," Sam suggested, like a child with no filter would.

I couldn't help but laugh, and my unladylike snort caught Ty's attention. He looked up and locked eyes with me, his arms still holding his weight on the back of the chair, and Sam still talking about football. I bit my bottom lip and tried to hide my smile, but seeing big bad Ty talking to little Sam was doing something to me.

"You a dancer?" Ty asked, and I straightened my back. Ty was anti-ballet when it came to being a man. He was probably one of those bullies in middle school who picked on the smaller kids who liked things he couldn't understand.

"Um," Sam was debating on how to answer Ty. He was clearly torn between saying yes in front of me, and playing it cool in front of Ty. His dance gear gave him away, though, and he realized it before he answered. "Yeah, kinda. Thinking about quitting for football."

I couldn't help the sadness that came over my face at his words. I looked to Sam's mom, who had the same sadness in her eyes as she watched her son chat with Ty. It was like a sign, Sam meeting Ty on the same day he debated leaving dance for football. I was going to lose my star student, my favorite little guy, my talented friend.

Ty was looking at me as he stood straight up and patted Sam's head. "As long as you do whatever makes you happy, little man. It's important to follow your dreams."

"I'm going to do a few more classes with Miss Metro and decide," Sam added.

"Dude, sounds good. Maybe I'll see you here again then."

"Wait, what are you doing here?" Sam asked.

Ty's eyes got wide, and I could tell he wanted to lie through his teeth. His face turned a little shade of pink, and his jaw started ticking.

"I'm a friend of Giselle's," he finally said, motioning to me.

"Miss Metro?" Sam asked, probably never knowing my first name.

"Yep," Ty started nodding. "Gonna get a workout in with her before I head back to the training complex."

"Oh my God, I hope I get to see you again, then!" Sam was jumping as his mom was telling him to calm down. She was asking Ty for a picture of him and Sam and trying to get her other son to join. She called him Reggie, and he barely even moved the whole time, clearly not caring about Ty's presence. Or anything, for that matter.

Other than Reggie being withdrawn, it was a happy moment for a little boy like Sam, on a day that was filled with such distress for his young heart. That thought alone gave me a reason to smile and be thankful for Ty.

He didn't discourage Sam from dancing, and he didn't discourage him from playing football. *"Follow your own dreams,"* was his sentiment, and no matter what Sam chose to do, as long as he followed his own dreams, I would be happy for him.

After the pictures were taken, they all left, and Ty and I were alone. It was the first time, apart from when I met Ty, that he was seeing my guard slip from a burst of emotions that I couldn't contain. So I turned around and headed back into the studio to get ready for Ty's class.

Behind me, I heard Ty taking his shoes off but I wasn't ready to turn around yet and start. It didn't feel like it was just an emotional evening with Sam. It felt like everything around me was too much to hold up on my own two shoulders. It felt like the moment I would break if I let myself show an ounce of weakness.

I couldn't do that.

After a few more deep breaths, I turned around, looking Ty directly in the eyes. His shoeless feet had gotten him closer to me than I realized. He was a foot in front of me, analyzing my face, and tilting his head.

I was going to clap and suggest we get started, but before I could, Ty closed the small distance between us and wrapped his arms around my body. And shocking both him and myself, I didn't fight it.

CHAPTER ELEVEN

LIKE ALWAYS, I waited to make sure everyone left *Brise* before I went in. Unfortunately, when I opened the door on Thursday, there was an older, heavy-set woman standing with her hands on her hips, watching inside the studio window intently, and a teenager slumped in the back of the reception area looking at his phone. I wanted to back away and wait it out, but she turned her head and smiled, so I was busted anyway. I figured I might as well wait inside the air conditioning for Giselle.

I nodded to the woman, ignored the teenager, and made my way to the back wall where the storage cubbies were. Once I leaned back, I was able to see Giselle squatting and holding on to one of her students—a boy, maybe in middle school.

She was focused on him and didn't even see me, but I could tell she was upset. It was the most emotion I had seen from her since we met. That included the time she screamed at me to leave.

"My boy," the lady said out loud without looking at me. "He's such a natural, and Miss Metro knows it. I know it. He knows it."

I wasn't sure if she was talking to me or to the other kid in the room, so I stayed quiet, but I made sure I paid attention to her in case she looked back at me for a response. She never did, but I could tell she was upset.

Giselle said a few more things to the boy before letting him go. As she stood, she looked up and saw me standing there, watching. I could tell the boy saw me and recognized me, but I kept my focus on Giselle for a minute longer.

I wanted to bust her balls and knock her off her pedestal a bit, but I realized that I probably never could. Not if that was her look of defeat. I didn't like it, I wanted to erase it. I hadn't even spoken to her yet, but I already missed her shoulders pulled back, and her eyes focused and stern. She walked toward the door, but she wasn't on her toes and gliding the way she normally was.

I was trying to refocus on the boy in front of me, who told me his name was Sam and that he was a huge fan of mine. Despite the fact that he was a ballet dancer, I saw a lot of myself in Sam. Maybe that was a quick judgment, but Sam was thin, too thin. He was wearing socks with holes, and his shorts were two sizes too big.

The difference was that Sam seemed to have people who cared about him. He may not have had money, or nice things, but his mom was there with him, caring about him. She had introduced herself while Sam rambled and Giselle watched on.

When Sam told me he was thinking of leaving ballet for football, I almost high-fived him and yelled, "Hell yeah." But that didn't feel right. I knew it was the reason Giselle was upset, and his mom didn't seem happy about it either.

I didn't lie to him either, though.

Honestly, I didn't know what Sam really wanted to do, but if he really did want to play football, why not? If he wanted to dance, he should. So I told him to be true to himself before taking a few pictures and saying goodbye.

It was only five minutes of knowing him, but I liked Sam a lot. I wanted to know how his story ended, and I made a note to come in a little earlier next week so I could see him in action for a few minutes.

By the time Sam left and Giselle walked back into the studio, her shoulders were still sagging, and her feet were flat. I followed her in quietly and tried to gauge how I should approach her.

Should I say something?

Fuck, I was so out of my element.

All of a sudden, I was praying she would snap at me and tell me how poor my form was, how much I sucked, and to call her Miss Metro.

I got closer to her, drawn by some unrecognizable need to see if she was okay. I was just about to say something when she turned around and tried showing me a stern look, one that said she was ready to be Miss Priss again.

But I wasn't ready.

And her stern look fell flat.

On instinct, I circled my arms around her, and to my surprise, she folded into my hold.

"I don't know what's wrong, but how can I fix it?" It didn't even faze me how out of character I sounded.

She shook her head back and forth against my chest, shaking a little from the emotions. She was trying to hold back tears that had most likely surfaced the moment I hugged her.

"What's wrong, Miss Priss?" I asked gently, running a hand soothingly over her back.

The use of my nickname for her made her laugh a little, and I swelled with some strange gratification over that small sound. It was also just the reprieve she needed to straighten her shoulders and lift her chin.

She backed away and looked up into my eyes. Hers were still glassy from unshed tears, and I tucked my hands behind my back to keep from catching them if they fell.

"Sam is special," she finally said, her voice strained but

controlled. "He got picked on today for being a dancer, and now he wants to quit."

"Oh shit," I breathed.

"I don't know if I am more upset that I may lose my star student, or that Sam is being bullied."

"Being bullied is rough, it changes us," my words were barely a whisper as my own memories resurfaced. I was always messed with for being poor, how messed up my parents were, and who my brother was. I was bigger and tougher than Sam, and I fought my bullies with fists and feet until they realized I wasn't the one to fuck with.

But it still changed me.

"I just want the best for him," she sniffed before shaking the rest of her emotions off and stepping back onto her toes. "Let's get started now."

She clapped twice and turned to the phone that controlled the music. Without a word, she turned on the soft beat that we used for the classical walk and I started prancing across the studio without having to be told.

As much as I wanted to fuck with her, it wasn't the time. Plus, I had taken the focus she gave me on my toes and used it in practice the last two days. It really did help, and who was I to fuck that up? We had our first preseason game Sunday, and I would do anything to keep the commentary off my poor play.

Our time went over our normal hour because we started late. It was like Giselle had a mental timer for exactly one hour, so I just kept at it until she called it quits.

In addition to the classical walk, she introduced a leap into the mix. Oddly enough, I saw that coming in handy, and wondered why I had never thought to leap with that same momentum and angle before. You would think jumping to catch a ball would be something a player thought about and focused on, but the truth was we mostly just ran on autopilot. We never overanalyzed our leaps until we sucked so bad it was what we had to do.

I started to think of some excuse to walk her home. I could always tell her I had to visit Coach again, but I realized she was keeping in touch with him and may not believe me. It ran through my mind that I could always park in front of her building, and then I wouldn't have to make an excuse.

It would look funny for me to park that far away, but I could. I probably would. For tonight, I was going to at least tell her I did, so I had the excuse. I didn't know what else she had going on, but added to the emotions with Sam, I wasn't going to feel right with myself unless I made sure she got home okay.

Call me crazy.

Call me old school.

Call me whatever, but I was four times the size of her, and if she was scared, there wasn't a chance in hell she didn't feel a little at ease with me hanging around.

"Um," she started to catch my attention as I tied my shoes. I was sitting in the reception area in a chair and looked up at her waiting by the door. I looked up quickly, too, because Miss Priss didn't use words like, *UM*. "Do you need to visit Mr. Peyton again?"

I stood up and angled my head, her eyes not quite meeting mine. "No," I said truthfully despite the fact that I was willing to lie to her three seconds before.

"Oh ok, cool."

Oh ok, cool? What the fuck, Miss Priss?

"I did have to park over there, though, so I'm headed that way. You need me to stop by and see him for any reason?"

"No, of course not, just wondering if you were going to head that way. I have some things I could use help carrying." No, she didn't. She was as packed up and ready to go as I was, and nothing in her hands was something she needed help with.

"Where is it? I can help."

"Oh never mind, I can get it tomorrow." *Sure Miss Priss.*

I nodded and smirked, silently calling her bluff. She looked a little pink and turned around to unlock the door so we could leave. Outside, she closed up while I waited, and we made our way across the park to her building.

"Thank you for what you said to Sam," she tucked a hair behind her ear that wasn't even there because her hair was spun up so tight. The motion gave away her nerves, though, and I was finding it pretty endearing. "It was kind of nice seeing you... less jerky."

A laugh escaped my mouth and it felt so fucking good. She had me all mixed up, and the whiplash was real.

"Not very often I lower the jerk level," I teased back. Which wasn't so much of a tease because it was true. "Kind of nice seeing you lower the *priss* down a notch."

She smiled quickly and then steeled her jaw, "Do not get used to it."

"Back at ya. As soon as you get your shit together, I'm going back to giving you shit."

Her smile returned but she stayed quiet, looking down at her feet as she walked. She was still in her ballet shoes and tights, a jacket thrown over her leotard for the smallest amount of modesty.

I swallowed hard, wanting to ask her what her deal was. I wanted to know why she rushed home, why she watched her back, why she kept her nose tilted up and her body ridged.

There were other things I wanted to know too. Things that were a little more unsettling. For instance, I wanted to know if she liked football, what she did for fun, and if she was dating anyone.

I shouldn't have cared, but I really wanted to know.

We reached her building, and she smiled before opening the main door. "Your car isn't over here, is it?"

One side of my mouth went up, giving myself away before I

could even speak. Truthfully, I didn't know what I should say, so maybe it was best that she saw straight through me.

"Thank you, Ty," her lips thinned in a smaller smile, but it had the same effect on me as the one she gave me earlier. She entered the building with no response from me but I waited and watched through the glass until she was safe inside the elevator.

I walked back to my car, suddenly excited for next Tuesday. I was looking forward to my ballet lesson just to see if Miss Priss was back in her standard uptight form.

First, I had to power through our first preseason game and hope I didn't fuck it up.

giselle

I TRIED GETTING BETTER about locking the door to the studio, even when class was in session.

I sometimes let it slip, though.

The police had informed me there were a few more reported incidents like mine on Friday evening, across town. No one was ever fatally injured so I wondered if they were taking it as seriously as I hoped they were. They assured me they were, so all I could do was go about my normal routines and hope nothing happened in the meantime.

Thankfully, it was Sunday, and I was home for the day, so I had nothing to worry about. The bad part was I had to call my mother.

I loved my mom, I really did. But I broke her heart when I left New York and the big stage. I thought opening a studio would make her happy, and it eased her a little that I was not completely turning my back on ballet. She wanted me on the stage, like her, though.

She no longer danced full time, but she was the great Galena Metrovik. If she wanted to dance, she did, and the people around her bent over backward to make it happen. I was supposed to be her legacy and the act she contributed to the arts once she was no longer a performer.

When I left, she cried, worried that the family name would never be known on the stage again. It was hard to explain to her that in a community that she was so revered in, I was the shadow. I was expected to be as good as she was, as perfect as she was.

Don't get me wrong, I was gifted beyond measure, and I knew it. Somehow, I could never outperform the expectations, though. Oftentimes, I was belittled by my peers who thought I only got the parts I did because of who my mother was, and I never knew if that was true.

I didn't stick around long enough to find out.

After battling mental breakdowns, body issues, and a sudden wave of stage fright, I walked out. I spent a month with my mom in her New York apartment, trying to feel better. We talked out the issues, and I saw a doctor. She and I both thought that, eventually, I would return to the stage.

But after that month, I ventured out to a bar with the one friend I knew I had in New York. We were reuniting after my breakdown, and that was supposed to be a celebration of my resurgence.

After a few drinks, I noticed a map on the wall, and people were throwing darts at it. The sign above it said, "You are here," with a big red dot over New York City. Below it, there was a sign that said, "Now, where are you going next?"

I walked over, entranced by the idea, and wondered if everyone who threw a dart really visited, or went where their dart landed. When I asked for a turn, my friend laughed and said it sounded like fun, but I took it as a sign. I'd already considered the idea of moving and starting over. I had even dreamt of staying with ballet and everything I knew, but using the talent in other ways—like owning my own studio. So I closed my eyes and threw the dart.

Before opening my eyes, I said to myself that the city closest to my dart (because I was not a small-town kind of girl) would be where I would go.

The dart landed on Ty Ty, Georgia.

As I sat there staring at the ceiling of my Atlanta apartment, and thinking back on that day, the irony was mind-blowing. Ty Ty, Georgia was directly in between Atlanta and Jacksonville, FL, but I never considered Jacksonville because the dart was in Georgia and I was going to stay true to the dart.

After that night out, I broke the news to my mom and she cried. But once she stopped, she hugged me and told me she wished me well. I hadn't seen her since, but not because I didn't want to. Opening and running a business was time-consuming and hard. I had dedicated my last year to being successful in Atlanta.

Mom had yet to come visit and I was assuming a part of that was being in denial. Despite her well wishes, I knew she was hurt. It was time to find out if her visiting was possible because I needed to call and ask her to come to Atlanta for our December show.

Picking up my phone, I nervously hit my mom's name, not daring to use FaceTime since I was not put together the way I knew she hoped I would be.

"Darling?" she answered with her perfect enunciation.

"Hello, Mom," I hoped my happy response didn't sound as fake as it felt. "How are you?"

"Good, good. Just left brunch with Marie and Antonia." She spoke like I knew them, but I didn't. Chances were, she didn't know them well either. Mom was a sucker for stuffy Sunday brunches with affluent people that attended her shows.

"Are you dancing right now?"

"No dear, just thinking about filling in for the lead in *La Bayadere*. You know I can do that with my eyes closed, but just not sure yet."

She really could. Most would think the life of a prima ballerina ended at a younger age, and that was most likely true since the average age of a dancer was thirty.

Galena Metrovik was the exception to the rule. She was only 45 years old and did not look a day over 30. She got pregnant with me when she was nineteen. She was attending The Vaganova School in St. Petersburg, Russia. Her parents were from there, and had sent her because they knew how good she was.

They didn't expect her to get pregnant, and honestly, I think my mom would have aborted me if she was not in a foreign country and had known how to go about it over there. Instead, she didn't tell a soul—not even my father. She was close to graduating and decided to hide the pregnancy as long as she could until she returned home to the United States.

She often joked that I was dancing before I was ever born and I guess that was true. Without a father, I was given her last name and thankfully, my grandparents helped her raise me while she climbed in her career. It wasn't until they passed away when I was nine that I lived with my mom full-time.

They left my mom all their money and assets, and it made living her dream and raising me possible. I always admired my mom when I was growing up. She taught me a lot, and took the time to ensure I always had what I needed. But she never gave up her own dream.

When she realized I had her talent, she made sure I had all the same opportunities she'd had. I attended top-notch dance schools, and climbed to the top quickly.

All it took was two years on stage in New York to realize I had been living her dream, and not my own. That I was not cut entirely from the same cloth as she was.

"Are you ok, dear?" she asked, cutting into my silent trip down memory lane.

"Yes, of course," I cleared my throat. I knew being poised and proper was a requirement from Galena. In the world of dancing, losing your poise was the same as losing your dignity. I may slip at times but I refused to slip in front of her.

"What do I owe the pleasure of your call? It has been weeks."

"It has, I apologize. I have been industrious with *Brise*. I have a wonderful, advanced class." I debated on whether I should mention the work with Ty, but I was sure she would scoff, and encourage me to steer clear of anyone who played such a barbaric game.

"That is wonderful. Are the finances in good standing?"

I blanched because that was a tough question. A part of me wanted to tell her it was none of her business, the other part of me felt she deserved to know since she had helped me get on my feet with the apartment. Plus, she was most likely worried about how I was doing, and money was essential to staying in business.

"I am good." Again, I left out the part about Mr. Peyton paying me a pretty penny to help Ty. "In fact, that is one reason I am calling. We have our first recital coming up in December, and I would love it if you joined us."

"Oh dear, that sounds…" I waited and prayed she would say yes. It made no difference to me, but I had to hold up my end of the bargain and provide a celebrity for the show. "….Dreadful," she finished.

"It would just be a small appearance. After all, everyone's parents here know of the great Galena Metorvik. It would be a thrill for them to meet you."

"I absolutely abhor children, you know that." She wasn't lying. Apart from me, she'd steered clear of kids my entire life. She didn't know how to speak to them, how to be warm to them. The only reason I was different was because I was her child, and she could mold me to fit her personality and way of life.

"These are great kids, amazingly talented. Your presence could play a small role in the success of a future star."

"Oh, Giselle. Darling. Let me think about that for a while. I am usually dancing around Christmas and I need to be sure I can clear my schedule. I am sure you understand?"

I did. I knew I was asking my mom to do something completely out of her comfort zone. We had actually discussed situations just like it when I left the stage, and she told me she had her own discomforts she battled with. She understood, to an extent.

"Of course, Mom. If you cannot make it, I completely understand. I would be a fool not to ask you, though."

"Never hurts to ask, darling," she breathed.

We spent the next hour catching up with each other, and having a rather pleasant conversation. My initial anxiety over speaking to her ebbed, and I was able to fill her in on a few more things about *Brise*. Although I left out the trouble with the break-in, and the presence of Ty Black.

I mentioned Sam, and despite her aversion to kids, she gave me great advice on how I should help him, and ways I could lure him back into dance. I had to start by showing him support for things he found interesting. He needed to see the good, bad, and ugly of whatever he was inspired by.

We hung up the phone, and as much as I usually dreaded those calls, I felt lighter than I had in a long time, so I decided to skip my workout and find something to watch on TV instead. It was not something I normally did, but it felt good to do something different. I flipped around the channels for a bit before stopping and sitting up quickly at what I was seeing.

The Atlanta Jets were playing the San Francisco Anchors in their first preseason game, and Ty's face was on the screen. His helmet was in his hand, his hair was a mess, and the profanity coming out of his mouth was obvious, even without being able to hear him.

"Black is not happy, and rightfully so. He may not have started it, but he threw the first punch, and that is an automatic ejection."

"And a fine."

"You're right about that. He's going to have to keep his cool this season, or teams will target his temper on purpose just to get him off the field. He may be struggling this preseason, but he's not going to stay that way long. He will be a target."

"He was already looking better today. He looked lighter on his feet. Now he sits the rest of the game in the locker room."

The announcers were breaking down everything that happened before I tuned in, and I sat in shock that the same man who spent time in my studio, classical walking and leaping, was the same man I saw on TV. Not to mention, that was the same guy who made excuses to walk me home out of some gallant nature.

He was different from the Ty I saw at his practice, as well. Nothing that I saw was what I expected to see when I turned on that TV.

All sides of Ty were hot, sexy, and enticing. I was cold and controlled, but I was also a woman. Ty was the epitome of a sexy alpha male, and there was no way I could lie if I was ever asked what I thought about him. It took all of my control to stay professional with him.

But the Ty that was slamming his helmet and threatening the female referee that was on the sidelines was making me feel things that were hard to control. I was both turned on, and jealous. I wanted to lose control like that, just once. I wanted to slam things and feel passionate enough to yell and scream.

With a pulse fluttering between my legs, I slid my fingers down and rubbed just enough to release the tension. It had been over a year since I had been with someone, so I chalked up the sudden feeling to the stress and solitude. I told myself that it wasn't Ty. He was just the first man I had spent any time with in a while, and I needed to ease a natural ache.

Suddenly, skipping the gym seemed like a terrible idea. It was a good way to ease any lust that consumed my body, and I was just about to get up when they showed Ty one more time.

Up close.

His tongue was running over his top lip as he was escorted to the tunnel that led to the locker room. He was covered in sweat and dirt, the black under his eyes was smudged. He hadn't shaved and had more scruff on his face than normal.

He looked like a villain. A menace.

Trouble.

But just as he made it to the entrance to the tunnel, he leaped with his toes pointed and back leg straight, just like I had taught him. It made me feel something else. Something deeper.

Slipping my hands under my waistband, I felt the rush of wetness from my pussy as I reacted to Ty. I gave up trying to fight the need, and rubbed myself quickly, giving myself an intense orgasm. It didn't take much because I was spun so tight, and once I let it go, I screamed, just like I had wished I could moments before.

Just like Ty.

Because of Ty.

CHAPTER THIRTEEN

I SLAMMED the door to my apartment, not even the slightest bit happy to finally be home. That may have been because I saw my brother lounging on my couch. Or it could have been I wanted to be back at that stadium, beating the fuck out of the guy who grabbed my face mask and slammed my head down. Funny how the refs didn't see that part, but the second I defended myself, I got tossed out of the game.

"I thought I told you to leave?"

"I didn't know when you would be back," he answered without even looking at me. He lifted the remote to turn the channel and took a drag from his cigarette.

"Doesn't matter when I come home, I told you to leave before I went to camp." I slammed my bags down and stalked to the fridge, looking for my protein drinks. There was nothing in the fridge but beer, so I slammed that shut, too. "You can't even replace the shit you drink? You even bother cleaning your shit out of the toilet?"

"Dude, chill out. It isn't even me you're mad at," he laughed but still never looked my way.

Rounding the bar that separated the kitchen and the living

room, I stalked toward the couch where Mike was sitting. He had switched the TV to the highlights of the game, and in big print was *Ty Black In Danger of Suspension*. The volume was down, but I knew the commentary that went with it was full of shit the people on TV didn't even know about.

"He could have given you a concussion," Mike said as I sat beside him. "You did what you had to do."

Leaning back, I breathed a sigh of frustration. I should have been picking him up and shoving him out the door, but I didn't have the energy. Mike was going to have to be dealt with another day.

"I'm so fucking tired," I confessed. "Camp and being attacked in the media. Coach has me doing some extra shit as well. I just need to sleep in my own damn bed."

"Go ahead, little bro. Marcus and Devon are out of town, so it's just me, and I swear I won't bother you."

"Out of town?" I leaned up and looked over to him.

"Yeah," he rolled his tongue around in his mouth, an excuse to stall what he wanted to say next. "Just had to take care of some business. You know."

As much as I wanted to be kept in the dark, I knew what their business was. I didn't participate, and it was the main reason they needed to move away from Atlanta—away from me. Mike would do anything to use my face for his so-called business. Just like any other company that used athletes to push their products, Mike wanted to use me to push drugs.

"Buy this shit, even Ty Black approves."

Fuck, he would be all over that if I let him. Maybe he already was and I just didn't know about it. Coach would make me die a very slow and painful death if he thought that was the case. My thoughts always worried about shit my brother did that hadn't actually happened yet. He made me crazy.

"You gotta leave, bro," I said calmly, hoping it sunk in. "Not just my apartment but Atlanta."

"No can do. We have things going on here. We need to see it through. Atlanta is a goldmine."

I breathed out hard again and shook my head, accepting the loss. If Mike deemed it a goldmine, he wouldn't ever leave. Not even the love of his little brother would make him leave good money.

"Find a new place to live, then. If it's a goldmine, you can afford your own place."

"Working on it. I swear. I'll be out by the end of the week."

Accepting his word, because I was too tired, I made my way to my room. It had been two weeks since I had been in there and I took a quick minute to make sure my shit was still in its place.

There wasn't much in my apartment. Most of my personal awards and things were in storage but I kept my Super Bowl rings in my drawer and that was the first thing I looked for.

Still there.

For a minute, it hit me how stupid I was to leave them where Mike and his friends could find them. But realizing they were safe made me feel bad for thinking he would steal something I coveted.

Mike was bad news, but I *was* his brother. It was why it was so hard to make him leave all summer.

Maybe he did have a new place in the works and I needed to give him more credit. We lived in different worlds, but we came from the same place, and he always had my back. He wouldn't intentionally hurt what I love.

Feeling more at ease, I hopped in the shower and leaned back, letting the water rush over my head and shoulders. I was content with the realization that things weren't so bad. Mike was probably not going to hurt me, or my career. I also didn't play terribly before I got kicked out of the game. Then, to add a cherry on top, I got to see Giselle soon.

My eyes popped open, shocked I had added Giselle to my train of thought. It was true, though. I was looking forward to seeing her on Tuesday. It was already in my plans to park in front of her building, making sure there was no way we wouldn't walk together afterward.

Smiling to myself, I thought about the shit I was going to say to get under her perfect porcelain skin. A few insults and some name calling and she would be clenching that jaw trying to keep from losing her precious poise.

My body was reacting to the thought of being with her. I could feel the blood pumping through my veins and into my cock. There was a knot forming in my stomach and I shook my head, trying to erase the way my body was reacting.

As much as I thought it would be fun to fuck around with my ballet teacher, Coach would kill me. He would trade me straight to Cleveland, to a team with no hope, and no future. I knew better than to fuck around with his plans, and trying to unravel Miss Priss was definitely risking too much.

But that didn't mean I couldn't think about it.

Taking hold of my cock, I squeezed, relieving a little pressure while simultaneously getting myself ready for more. Leaning forward, I placed my other hand on the tile and stroked as my thoughts went deeper, darker, and dirtier.

More than anything, I wanted Miss Priss to lose her proper disposition, for her perfection to fall. But for the sake of my hard cock and my hot shower, I thought about her losing that control on me, with me. Her hair down, out of its tight bun. Her little skirt shoved up, giving me access to a pussy that was probably as tight as she was.

My cock would barely fit in her little cunt. I'd have to push hard, making her scream out, crying my name while crying.

"Fuck," I hissed to myself, slamming a hand on the tile. My movements got quicker, losing rhythm as I got closer to coming. The tingle down my back, the tension in my legs. I was ready to explode, so I opened my eyes and watched my hand stroke.

Biting my lip and suppressing a loud grunt, I came hard as

cum coated the wall in front of me. I looked at the mess and wondered why it didn't make me feel better. All I felt was unsatisfied.

Monday was the first day I'd had off in weeks.

No practice, no camp, no game, no ballet, no nothing. Even Mike had texted me and said he would be gone for a while.

A part of me wanted to lay in my bed all day and celebrate by doing nothing. The other part of me wanted donuts. There were a million donut shops near my side of town and I could have chosen any of them. They would have suited me just fine.

However, I ended up on a bench in Centennial Park, a donut from The A-hole in my hand, and a perfect view of *Brise*.

Yes, I felt creepy. And yes, I realized I was crossing a line that should have been erased by seeing my cum all over my shower. Yet, there I sat, wondering what time Giselle went to work, and what she wore to work in the daylight, when it was harder to hide her tutu.

Taking a bite of my donut, I scanned the sidewalks and stopped when my eyes hit a familiar face. Not Giselle, but Mike, walking quickly with his head down and hands in his pockets. He was out of place and I was even more confused when he stopped in front of *Brise* and tried opening the locked door.

I stood up, about to call his name and ask him what the fuck he was doing, but before I could, he ran. There was a nail salon a block over and I watched as he darted into the door, looking back to see if anyone saw him.

What in the actual fuck?

Frozen in place, I held my hands slightly out, pinching my

donut between two fingers. Why was Mike trying to go in *Brise*? Did he know Giselle?

That didn't make sense.

There wasn't even time to wonder too much about it before Giselle went scurrying past me. She was wearing leggings and a tank top and had a few bags in her arms. If it wasn't for her hair being in its perfect bun, I'm not sure I would have noticed it was her so quickly.

"Hey, hey." I jogged to catch up to her and grabbed some bags from her hand. "Let me help."

Her eyes shot up and even though she had started to pull away, she gave the bags up easily when she saw it was me. "Mr. Black, thank you."

I rolled my eyes at her and held on to the bags as she approached the door to *Brise*. She fumbled for a key, but had the door unlocked in no time. She held it open for me, inviting me in with her bags, but right before I entered, I looked back at the nail salon my brother went into.

He wasn't getting a mani/pedi, he was already back on the sidewalk.

Staring at me.

Anger in his eyes.

giselle

BEING LATE WASN'T ACCEPTABLE, but it was Monday so I tried to give myself grace. It was hard to be upset when I slept better that night than I had in a year. Never mind the reason being the fact that I eased the tension in my body to an image of Tyson Black—the man standing in front of me, offering to help me with my bags.

"Please come in." I used my professional tone to try and hide how embarrassed I was about what I had done. Even if he had no idea, I knew, and I felt the humiliation coursing through me.

Ty had been frozen outside the door, looking off at something, or someone. My words snapped his eyes up to me and he entered, a little bit shaken, like he had seen a ghost.

"Everything okay?" I tilted my head, seriously concerned for a minute.

"Um, yeah, I guess." He set my bags down on the desk and looked around like he wasn't sure where he was.

"What are you doing here?"

"I was having breakfast in the park when I saw you running with the bags," he shrugged, but was still looking around aimlessly. "Figured I would give ya a hand."

"And you are sure you are okay?"

"Yeah," he finally laughed at himself and shook the uncertainty from his expression. "I thought I saw someone I knew."

By the look on his face, it wasn't someone he wanted to run into. An ex-girlfriend, perhaps.

"Well, I appreciate you being in the right place at the right time. See you tomorrow for class?"

"How's Sam?" He didn't take my hint that he could leave, and instead, took me by surprise with this question. He seemed to be genuinely interested, and his concern warmed my heart a little.

"I have not seen him since last Thursday. I did think of a few ways to help him, though."

"Oh, how?"

"Not sure how I am going to do it, but I want to be his friend. Someone that he knows supports him no matter what. I just have to see if I can do that, being that I am his dance teacher, and not a student in his school."

"Seems complicated, Miss Metro."

My name rolled off his tongue with sarcasm, but his tone deepened and his eyes were boring into me. I started to flush as I remembered him from the TV, looking angry, untethered, and manic. How was he the same person?

"Well, I know it is not ideal, but if I want to be influential in his life, I need to be more than his instructor."

"Is that legal? Or proper? Or whatever else?"

"I do not plan on luring him to my car with candy."

Ty laughed and shook his head, "Yeah, well. I was a young boy once. Trust me. Sam may not be able to read between those lines."

"What is it you think I have planned for poor Sam? Back row at the movies? Late night picnic at make out point?"

"What else is there?"

"Football."

Ty's eyes got wide, and he looked both impressed and confused.

"I will chat with him about football instead of ballet. I will ask him to tell me what he likes about it, and show him that I am invested in his happiness. Because I *am* invested in his happiness."

"Do you know anything about football?"

"I know enough."

"Tell me something...anything." He crossed his arms, challenging me to run off some football rules or plays. Or maybe he thought I would give him some basics—field distance, a position —or use the word touchdown.

Instead, I smirked a little and crossed my arms, mirroring him. My entire persona faded as I smirked with a gleam in my eye. "I know that when someone grabs your helmet and slams your head down, you're supposed to get up and punch them."

His smile fell and his eyes darkened. *Was that too much? Did I go too far?*

We stayed like that for a full minute as he stared daggers into me. He finally pursed his lips and flared his nose. "You watched my game?"

"I saw *that* part," I admitted.

"He had it coming," he defended himself but there was no need. Maybe he thought of me as soft and dainty, unable to fathom punches being thrown, but I knew when a punch was warranted.

"He did," I nodded. "My only concern was a broken hand and a concussion setting back your arabesque."

Ty snorted and dropped his defenses at my words. He ran a hand through his messy hair and it was only then that I started realizing he was in jeans and a t-shirt, no hat. Every time I had seen him before, he was in gym clothes, ready to workout, with his hat on backward.

Ty in plain clothes was another level of material for my brain on nights I needed to give myself pleasure. I wouldn't deny myself that.

As Ty was staring at me, analyzing me, his eyes were darting around my face, looking for God knows what. I felt vulnerable and exposed for a minute, like the ice I coated myself with every morning was melting away with the heat of his stare.

I couldn't let that happen. So I did what I did best and clapped twice, breaking the spell. "In the studio for an extra lesson, or out."

Ty looked at the window with the dance floor behind it and then back to me. For a minute, I thought he was about to call my bluff and choose option A. But he held his hands up in surrender and backed away.

"You win, Miss Priss. As much as I love the way we dance, I have a whole day of doing nothing to get back to."

"Thank you for the help," I nodded, my manners seeming important.

"Any time," he saluted me and back peddled out of the door.

I didn't want him to know I was going to rush behind him to lock the door. I didn't want him to assume I was scared—even though I was almost positive he was catching on because he kept walking me home.

However, I counted to ten and lunged toward the door, not breathing until I was sure I was safe. It took several breaths before I walked toward my office and as I entered, the phone started ringing and my day was officially underway.

"Hi Sam!" I greeted on Tuesday evening as he dragged his feet into the studio. He didn't look happy to be there, and my heart broke a little. I was hoping by the time I saw him again, he would have bounced back.

"Hi Sam!" I repeated, not accepting his moping as an excuse not to be polite.

"Hi Miss Metro," he mumbled. He had his eyes to the ground, taking his assigned spot on the floor.

With the entire class there, I couldn't take the time to chat with him about football, or anything else, so I was just going to have to wait until class was over.

We got to work on the different sections for our recital and separating the parts. I then went to each group and gave them a dance to practice. Since it was my advanced class, they all knew the steps, and just needed to be able to perform them in the correct order for the individual songs.

It made being the only teacher in the studio easier.

Luckily, the excitement over the recital was still propelling the kids to be on their best behavior, and to practice hard. Class went smoothly, and before I knew it, my mental clock was telling me class was over.

Once I clapped a couple of times and told the class they did well, I sent them out of the studio. I wanted to tell Sam to wait for me but he was running out of the studio quickly, excitement in his eyes.

"You're back!" He yelled, making me look out of the window to the reception area.

Ty was smiling and leaning his elbow on the counter where the receptionist sat when she was in. He was talking to Sam's mom and she was trying not to swoon. Her hand was to her chest, and she was laughing at whatever Ty had just said.

I slowly left the studio once everyone was gone, and watched on as Sam jumped to give Ty a high-five. Then I heard Sam scream with what I hoped was excitement and he started jumping up and down, pleading with his mom.

By the time I made my way out of the door to where I could hear them, Mrs. Watson was holding her hands up in surrender, "Okay, okay, we can go to the game."

Ty and Sam high-fived again while I crossed my arms, wondering what I had missed.

"Miss Metro, Ty just invited us to his game on Sunday. It's only preseason but that's okay, I've never been."

"Wow, invited?"

"Yeah, we get his special tickets, and get to go in the special gate."

Ty was smiling, satisfied with himself while I wanted to slice his throat. He knew how much I wanted to connect with Sam, he knew that I wanted him to dance. Yet, there he was, giving Sam the keys to the football field.

"That is exciting." I probably sounded pissed. Very, very pissed. There was no way I could compete with whatever Ty was going to treat him to.

"The best part is," Ty added, "Since Miss Metro and I are such good friends, she was already going to come. That means you will be sitting with her, and she won't be alone."

"Oh good, that is good news," Mrs. Watson smiled as she clapped her hands together, more pleased than ever that she had agreed to go.

Meanwhile, my eyes were as wide as saucers, confused as to how I got roped into a football game. I wanted to say, *"Um no."* But another part of me—a very, very small part—wanted to watch Ty play in person.

Without being able to speak properly, my silence spoke for me and everyone had arranged for us to meet at the players' Friend and Family entrance an hour before the start of the game.

While they finished talking, I walked behind the counter until Sam and Mrs. Watson were gone. It was a small way to distract myself from screaming, and avoiding going into the studio with Ty until I was calmer.

None of that lasted very long. Maybe thirty seconds after I heard the door shut. Then I spun around and eyed Ty in anger.

"How dare you!" He didn't say anything, just looked at me.

"You have no right showing up here and creating a situation that you know hurts me. You are deliberately doing this to piss me off, and guess what? Its fucking working."

Ty looked shocked, at my words, or the fact that I was losing my ever present poise. Either way, I couldn't stop yelling long enough to find out.

"I confided in you. I told you Sam was important to me. I told you he was the best dancer I had ever seen. I told you I wanted to help him, and I even told you how. How dare you do this to me."

What I said finally had Ty finding his voice and not holding back. "How dare me? This isn't about you, yet ironically it *is* for you."

"That doesn't even make sense!"

"What Sam chooses to do is not your problem. I understand that—"

"What Sam does is not your problem either. You barely even know him. Yet you swoop in here just in time to give him the passport to your world."

"My…? Do…? What?" Ty's head was spinning, I could see it as if it was on an actual stick and the wind was blowing in circles. I knew I was flying off the handle and giving him a lot to be confused about, but I had been so good.

So. Damn. Good.

I held myself to the highest standard, and always put on a professional front. I followed all the rules. I worked my ass off. I did extra shit, like teach football players how to focus and balance and leap, all to make extra money and get extra credit in the community.

All it took was a little interference from Tyson Black, and I felt out of control. Wild. If I was any less of a lady, I may have stormed up to him and yanked his perfect hair from his perfect head. Maybe even tried strangling him.

The past couple of weeks had been hell. I still had bruises on my face that I covered with makeup. I walked to work every day scared out of my mind that someone would storm inside *Brise* again and hurt me—or one of my kids. I put up with Ty. I mourned Sam's hardship. I all but begged my mom to come down for the recital.

Ty was about to be the poor soul that felt the wrath of Giselle Metrovik finally snapping. I felt good about it too, because he was the reason I was losing my handle on my emotions.

"Don't act like you aren't using Sam to piss me off. That's all this is. All you've done is work to get under my skin, and you found the worst way, didn't you?"

Ty tilted his head, still unable to speak, or comprehend what was going on. I didn't want to look at him, I didn't want him near me. I was about to yell at him to leave, but I never got that chance.

He had snapped back to his senses and was directly in front of me in two strides. He lifted me up and put me on the counter, positioning himself between my spread legs. It was my turn to be too stunned to talk, and with me on the counter, we were eye to eye. He got inches from my face and the snarl he gave me told me he was pissed.

"As fun as it is to see you fall the fuck apart, I had hoped the stick that is shoved up that ass would have vacated when you did. I have been trying to pull it out, but I sure as fuck haven't been trying to make you lose your goddamn mind."

I opened my mouth to speak but he grabbed my chin, using his thumb and pointer finger to purse my lips like a fish.

"I didn't plan on pissing you off like this. I didn't give Sam those tickets to lure him away from dancing. You told me yesterday you were gonna use football to befriend him, to chat with him. He obviously likes the Jets, so it slipped out to offer his mom and him some tickets. Something tells me they don't make it to too many games because its fucking expensive. So excuse me for helping that kid have the chance to do so."

I squinted my eyes, but knew he had a point. I had been so

wrapped up in my selfishness that I didn't even consider how lucky Sam was to get the chance. Ty somehow knew that the Watsons couldn't afford that luxury, and I should have been glad he was giving them the opportunity.

"Yeah, I overstepped when I told them you were going, but it all fucking fell into place and I didn't want to give you the chance to say no. You told me you wanted to connect with Sam and chat with him. You promised you wouldn't lure him with candy, so why not join him at the game? I thought it would be the perfect time for you to get into his little head and have that talk you told me about."

My breathing had softened and my shoulders had slumped. I was feeling myself come down from my tirade. I knew I was being irrational again. Ty seemed to be sincere, but I had been so stressed and ready to lose it on someone.

Ty had given me the perfect opportunity, and it seemed he was taking it away just as quickly.

"Yeah," I nodded, not worrying how unprofessional I sounded. Ty still had his body between my legs, my shoulders were slumped, and he had just put me in my place.

"Yeah?" he asked, not sure if he was hearing me correctly.

I nodded again and looked up into his eyes. Ty was only inches from my face. His hands were on my thighs, initially to hold me in place, but as we sat there staring at one another, his hands started slowly climbing toward my hips.

His soft touch was creating goosebumps on my skin, and I could tell he felt them by the way his lips quirked. For a moment, it felt like he was going to kiss me. All the makings of an amazing kiss were in play, and my body was giving away how good I felt with his hands on me.

Ty didn't seem like the kind of man that second guessed or questioned himself. He seemed like if he wanted it, he took it, so his hesitation almost had me back pedaling from his hold.

Almost.

There was still a part of me that buzzed for him. After the emotions I had been having, and all the ups and downs, it would be easy to convince myself that it didn't really matter who was there with me, that I would crave the attention and connection.

But that wasn't true. It was Ty I had used as my muse to give myself release. It was his angry and manic image that made me want to melt.

Hoping he took the hint, I licked my lips and closed the gap. If I had been braver and bolder, I would have kissed him first. But I had used all the energy I had to yell at him.

"Is that how I do it? Will that work?" One side of Ty's lips lifted in a small smile.

It was my turn to be confused. *Would what work?*

His hands went further up my legs, his thumbs close to the apex of my thighs. He squeezed harder, causing a small moan to escape my lips.

"Is this how I get that stick out of your ass, Miss Priss? Do I need to coax it out like this?" His thumb was softly rubbing my pussy on the outside of my leotard. So soft that I could barely feel it, but it was there, enough to make me want to move forward and press into him harder.

He was taking his cues from the way I was responding to him, and I knew I needed to nod if I wanted him to keep going. If he wanted to see me come undone, I was going to let him.

Moving my hips forward, I caused his thumb to apply a little more pressure and my hands went to his shoulders to give myself more leverage. I knew we were supposed to be dancing. It was what I was getting paid for, but whatever was happening was what I needed.

Just as I decided to wrap my legs around his waist and pull him closer, the front door opened and the lights went off.

"I'm back, bitch!"

CHAPTER FIFTEEN

I WAS GOING to kiss her. She knew it, I knew it.

Seeing her fired up and crazy was better than I could have ever imagined. Even if she was angry and pissed for no good reason, I was loving every second of it.

My cock was as hard as a goddamn rock, and when my thumbs subconsciously made their way to her pussy, I could feel the heat and dampness seeping through her tights. There had always been a charge of fireworks between us, but I had made peace with not fucking my dance teacher.

Now that I knew what kind of crazy she was capable of, I wanted to see it without the tutu on.

I was still on the same mission—to make her wild—but I wanted to do it a different way. I gave her a lot of chances to say no. I waited long enough for her to tell me to back the fuck up while I hinted at my intentions. Not once did she flinch.

So fuck whatever she was to me, and fuck the fact that Coach would kill me. Miss Priss needed to be unwound and I was up to the task.

Leaning in, my lips just about pressed to hers when a crash

into the front door stole all the anticipation and heat from the room.

The lights went out instantly, and a voice that sounded oddly familiar yelled, "I'm back, Bitch!"

Giselle screamed and without another thought, I picked her up and threw us both behind the counter onto the floor. I was hovering over her, hiding her, protecting her.

Even in the darkness, I could see her eyes wide and her mouth trying not to scream again. There were footsteps pacing back and forth in the main part of the reception area and I waited, wondering if they were going to come behind the counter and find us.

Since my back was to the door when it all happened, I never got to see who came in, or if they saw us. Giselle was so focused on my lips coming toward hers that there was no way she saw anything before the lights went out.

"I know you're in here," the man finally spoke. "It's about time you left the door unlocked. The next step was going to be to blow this place up. Don't make me fuck you up again."

It sounded as though it wasn't the first time this had happened, and I was wondering if Giselle knew the guy personally. Was it a domestic issue? How much danger was she in?

Preparing myself for a fight, I leaned up slightly off Giselle, but before the guy made a move, the door opened again and he was gone.

Just like that.

Giselle was curled into herself, struck with fear. Her body was shaking and her breathing was erratic.

Once I realized he really was gone, I raced to the door and locked it, before returning to Giselle and scooping her into my arms. She buried her head into my chest and held on tightly to the front of my shirt.

Kicking the back door, I found her office, and a couch in there where I sat down with her still in my arms and rocked her as if she were a child. I honestly didn't know what else to do. She was scared, I was confused, and we both needed a minute before either of us could talk.

"We need to call the police," I whispered and she nodded against my chest. I placed a kiss on her head before moving her to the couch and standing to pick up the phone from her desk.

"Call the number on the card," her voice was scratchy but I heard her and even found the card she was speaking off right on top of the phone. It was for a detective with the Atlanta Police Department.

I dialed the number and the officer on the other end picked up quickly.

"Miss Metrovik?" he said with a worried tone. "Are you okay?"

"This is Tyson Black, a friend of Giselle's. She told me to call this number to report someone entering and threatening her at the *Brise* dance studio."

"Fuck," he said under his breath before asking, "Was she hurt again?"

Again? Hurt?

"No, just shook up and scared."

"My partner and I are on our way."

I hung up and turned back to her, watching her shake on the couch. I got back to her as quickly as I could and placed her back into my lap where I could make her feel safe.

"This happened before?"

"Yes, a few weeks ago. I'm so sorry," she cried.

"Sorry for what? You didn't do anything."

"I brought you into this mess. I didn't lock the door. I should never have put anyone at risk." She was rambling, and I wasn't catching up quickly enough. All I knew was that we were okay, not hurt, nothing happened. We were scared, and as far as I was concerned, if there was a mess she brought me into, I was glad I was there and she wasn't alone.

Had she been alone, he may not have walked away, and that scared the shit out of me.

"I'm glad I was here. What happened last time?"

"The same thing, sort of," she bit her lip and looked up into my eyes. "He came in and paced, waited. Only last time, before he left, he got closer to me and hit me, knocking me out cold."

"Is this someone you know?"

She shook her head adamantly, telling me earnestly, and without words, that she had no clue who he was.

"Do you know what he looks like?"

"I saw him when he approached the first time. He got closer and I was able to see him briefly before he hit me. I woke up on the floor a few minutes later and he was gone. I called the police. They started investigating and...oh shit."

"What?"

"I'm just so sorry," she cried again.

It was official, Miss Priss was gone, and in her place was a scared, but strong woman, that spoke using cuss words and didn't finish her thought before thinking of something else. She was no longer speaking like a robot with a stick up its ass either.

Apart from the fear, I felt like I was seeing the real Giselle for the first time.

"Tell me what this is all about," I urged just as we heard a knock on the door.

Giselle stayed put on the couch as I approached the door, looking through the blinds first to make sure it was the detective. He brandished his badge when he saw me peek, and I opened the door.

"Thanks for coming so quick," I said, then introduced myself before leading them back to where Giselle was.

They asked her a couple of questions that I didn't understand, but she stayed with the flow and gave them what they needed. Then they turned to me.

"Mr. Black. First of all, I'm a huge fan. Second of all, what're you doing here?"

Cops or not, they were obviously fans, and I didn't want them knowing I was here for ballet lessons. No one but Giselle and Coach were ever going to find out. In fact, I would rather go to jail.

"I just stopped in to walk Giselle home. She's a friend of mine." There was enough truth in that to suffice, and Giselle didn't argue with me either.

"You're walking her home, but you seemed unaware this had happened before."

"Well, Giselle didn't tell me, that's for sure. But I still knew she needed a friend to walk her home."

He wrote some notes down, old school style in a little notebook with a pencil smaller than the one at the mini golf place. Both of them gave a few nods and hums before deciding they had asked all they were going to.

"Miss Metrovik, please let me know if you have any more trouble. We'll be placing a full time patrol on this road, and hopefully, this is the last time you have to face this."

She seemed happy about the patrol so I stayed quiet, but the meaner and more aggressive part of me considered slamming the guy into the wall and asking why he hadn't done that after the first time.

For her sake, I refrained, and walked them to the door to let them out before locking it again. When I made my way back to the office, Giselle was throwing things in a bag and putting a jacket on over her leotards and tights. She was fighting with the fabric, and seemed to be in a hurry, so I helped her before she had a complete breakdown.

We quietly locked the doors, and I took her hand in mine to walk her across the park to her building. It made a lot more sense why she was so scared, and why she ran every night without bothering to change her clothes.

"Just on the nights I'm here," the realization hit me.

Her steps stuttered and she squeezed my hand before nodding. "The night this first happened was the night I ran into Mr. Peyton in the lobby of our building. He had no idea what had happened. I ended up with a bruise on my cheek, but that night, it wasn't very prominent yet. He saw me in my attire and asked if I taught ballet, and the rest is history. He let me choose the day and time you came, and offered me payment. I accepted the money, but I really jumped on the idea of not being alone. I was scared, but I never imagined them returning, not until the detective showed up and told me it was a ring and may happen again. By then, you were already a student. I debated on closing down, but they told me just to keep my door locked."

"We didn't lock the door after Sam left, did we?"

She shook her head and looked to her feet as we kept walking.

"This is so fucked up," I breathed, looking at the sky. "What are you going to do?"

"I'll do a better job of locking the doors, and with the patrol cars around, maybe it won't happen again."

"What the hell do they want?"

"Just a place to hide, is what I was told. They seem to know the schedule I hold, too. I don't know if that is true, but the detectives told me it was likely they did their homework."

"They?" I was still shaking my head in disbelief. It all seemed like a game.

"I don't know, Ty," she breathed out my first name and shrugged. "I just don't fucking know."

"Hey," I tugged her hand and turned her to face me. We had just approached her building and were on the sidewalk. The light from the lobby was bright through the windows and I could see how worn out she was from the craziness of the night.

"You scared me the first night you came in," she confessed as I pulled her into a hug.

"I look scary," I admitted. "But there is nothing scary about a guy that does classical walking and leaps two nights a week. Trust me."

She released our hug and tried to smile as she backed up toward her door. "Want to cancel Thursday?"

"No."

"So you want to try again?"

Did she mean ballet, or the fucking we were about to do before all hell broke loose? It didn't matter. Either way, I would be there with my best socks on, and my pal Chase Turner's favorite baseball bat.

giselle

AS A PRECAUTION, I canceled all of my classes for the remainder of the week, and sent videos to the parents for their kids to practice at home. I didn't tell them why I was canceling, just that there was a personal issue. No matter how many times the detective told me that the odds were small that they would come in with kids in class, I didn't want to risk it anymore.

It was bad enough that I was there alone, waiting for Ty for our normal class. He was the one student I didn't want to cancel on, not only because the team was paying me, but because I wanted to see him again. I owed him another apology for getting crazy about Sam, and then putting him in a dangerous situation without telling him. For leading him on. For letting myself be unprofessional.

Without the kids in the studio, I took some time to dance my way. The way I did on stage for those few years. I started the music and loosened myself up, letting the stress and worry fall from my shoulders. Bending and rotating at the waist, I did a circle with my torso, creating a faster motion as I went.

Then the music got harder, and I leaped, feeling myself fly across the hardwood floor. I planted my foot as I landed and spun, creating a twirl with the skirt I had on over my capri-length leggings.

Paired with a tank top over my sports bra, it was a different look than my normal work attire. Ballerinas, even those of us who had retired from the stage, loved the twirl of a skirt on our hips.

Putting myself into a *pointe* on my right leg, I lifted my left leg until it was straight up next to my cheek. It had been a while since I had done any training outside of the classes with the kids, so I was beaming with self-satisfaction at my reflection in the mirror.

I dropped my leg down and kicked back, propelling myself into a *fouetté*. Spinning faster and faster, I challenged myself to stay balanced, focused, and poised. The music urged me on, making me want to spin forever.

To dance forever.

When I slowed down and stopped to catch my breath, I looked into the mirror at my flushed face. I walked away because I couldn't handle the pressure, yet, I was dying inside knowing an eleven year old was wanting to do the same thing. Maybe I was wrong for that, but I wanted him to be better than me. Stronger than me.

Movement in the mirror caught my eye, and I spun quickly to look into the reception area. Ty was standing there with his arms crossed over his chest and a look I couldn't distinguish on his face. I let out a sigh of relief that it was him, and started toward the door to the studio to invite him in. He was early, but I owed him some time, so there was no sense in making him wait any longer.

With my shoulders back and my professional air back in place, I tiptoed into the reception area and walked toward him.

"Good evening, Mr. Black," I smiled and nodded, stopping a few feet away from him. He never uncrossed his arms, his eyes got small and dark, and his lips pressed into a straight line.

Ty was angry, that much I could tell. So I tilted my head and creased my brow, silently asking him what was wrong. I prepared myself for a little bit of anger because of what I had subjected him to. I knew we needed to talk before we danced, but I fully expected him to be a little more professional about it.

An adult.

Yet, like a child, he never spoke, just eyed me and pouted.

"Is there a problem, Mr. Black?"

My words broke his stare and he closed the gap that separated us. Instinctively, I took a few steps backward, trying to keep the same distance between us. I wasn't far from the door to the studio so I backed in, and he kept following me.

Once we were both inside, he slammed the door shut and kept stalking toward me. Admittedly, I had never seen Ty like he was at that moment. Comparing him to a child was unfair because as he backed me further into the room, I realized he was more like an animal.

Despite someone just as large as him breaking into my business twice, and scaring the shit out of me, I wasn't scared of Ty. Maybe I should have been since I didn't know much about him on a personal level. But what I did know about him made me feel at ease and safe, even while being hunted.

Holding my hands up to slow him down, my back hit the barre that hung from the mirror on the wall. He stopped, but with his long arms, he reached out to grab my chin.

"Do not fucking call me Mr. Black. Don't start that shit, Miss Priss. You already let me see the curtain fall, and I sure as fuck do not want it closed on me again."

"What is under your skin, *Ty?*" I scoffed and pushed his hand away, unsure how to take his words. "You've only been here three minutes, what could I have possibly done in that short time frame?"

"Nine minutes," he growled. "I've been here nine minutes, Giselle. Nine. Want to know how I got in?"

My eyes widened because once he said the words, I knew how he got in.

"The fucking door was unlocked, Giselle. And as fucking amazing as it is to watch you dance, the music was up and you were in your zone, and I could have been any fucking body and you would have never known."

His fists were clenched and I could see him shaking. He was in his standard cut-off t-shirt and gym shorts. His shoes were still on, probably scuffing my floors but I wasn't crazy enough to bring that up.

Ty was right. Without the kids here, I walked right in and never looked back. I knew Ty would be coming, and I let locking the door slip my mind.

"Shit," I whispered, lowering my head. "I canceled classes for the week and waltzed right in here for the first time since we left Tuesday."

His hand found my chin again and he lifted my head up so he could look in my eyes. "Scared the shit out of me."

Without knowing what else could I say, I just nodded. Locking the door was rule number one, and we both knew it.

He dropped his hand from my chin and turned around, running both hands through his hair. He was shaken up, but I didn't realize how much he was affected by what happened until that moment.

"I am so sorry about what happened."

"There you go, apologizing again," he turned back to me quickly. "You ever gonna stop?"

Ty was confusing, and I wasn't sure who I was when he was around. It took everything I had to keep my shoulders pulled back and my head held high. He probably thought I was certifiable with the way I teetered back and forth, but he was the first person that had seen the many sides of Giselle Metrovik in a long time.

"Let's dance," I turned to face the mirror and held onto the barre in front of me. I could see Ty watching me in the reflection and we locked eyes.

The mirror was like a shield. He could see me, I could see him, but with my back to him, I was braver. It was easier to keep my head held high despite his eyes boring into mine.

After another few silent minutes, Ty approached me and put both of his hands on the barre, one on either side of me. He pressed his back against mine and lowered his mouth down near my ear. Our eyes were still locked in the mirror as he created a cocoon around me, making me feel secure and safe.

"I'll dance with you, Giselle, but I won't let you raise that prissy facade again. I know what I have to do break it down, and all I need is a hint of that uptight attitude to snap."

Lifting my chin, I made sure he was looking directly in my eyes before I said, "Your shoulders are sagging, your feet are facing different directions, and your face has a scowl, *Mr. Black.*"

Was I calling his bluff?

Testing him?

There wasn't time to consider why I did it before using the exact words I used to describe him the first day I met him. The same words that crawled under his skin on day one. I didn't mean to be insulting at the time, I was just doing my job and stating things we needed to address. But now I was intentionally digging under his skin hoping he took the hint.

I wanted his thumbs between my legs and his hands on my thighs. I wanted to feel how I felt right before the door busted in on us.

If I had to scream and yell again, I would because something about him was making me desperate.

Keeping his eyes still on mine, Ty lowered his lips to my neck and slowly licked, testing the waters. Tilting my head, I made sure he knew that was exactly what I wanted, and he took the extra space to flatten his tongue on my neck again.

A small moan escaped my mouth before my eyes started

closing in pleasure. Ty's hands left the barre and found my hips, holding me in place as he pressed his hard cock into my backside. I pressed into him and started to move slightly until he gave me a small growl.

Snapping my eyes back open, I watched him in the mirror as he took over the movement of my hips, grinding into me harder and harder.

"Start the music," Ty whispered.

Lifting off the barre, I reached to the table I kept my phone on and blindly scrolled my playlist. When I hit play on a random song, I dropped the phone to the floor, not caring how loud it was or if my phone was okay. I needed my hands back on the barre before I sunk to the ground from the need coursing in my veins.

Wicked Games by The Weekend started, and I knew it was a dirty trick by karma. Something so sexual, so lyrically accurate, playing while we moved against one another. If I had anything holding me back, that song was just enough to erase whatever it was.

"Lean up, baby," Ty whispered. "Dance with me."

Raising off the barre, I kept my body against his as he pulled us into the middle of the room. He continued to move against me, encouraging me to dance, so I started to move my hips, the way I had been moments before. Only that time, we moved in rhythm together, to the beat.

Ty wrapped his hands tighter around my waist, holding me so I could fall deeper against him. I laid my head back on his shoulder and closed my eyes, letting my body move however it wanted. We were dancing, swaying, and I could feel every part of me coming unraveled.

Without my one-piece leotard on, Ty found the sensitive skin of my stomach and started caressing me with the tips of his fingers. My hands fell on top of his and held them in place as a small moan once again escaped my lips.

Ty's breath was on my neck, even and controlled. Every so often, his lips would close in a kiss, or his tongue would taste my skin.

It wasn't until the song ended that the spell broke, but only for a second. Ty grabbed one hand and twirled me around so I was facing him, pulling me into his body, face to face. Instead of his hands back on my hips, he wrapped them around each side of my neck and brought my lips close to his, touching just slightly.

"This is so much better than pissing you off," he whispered. His tongue snaked out and tested the seam of my lips before retreating. "You're going to let me kiss you, aren't you?"

I nodded quickly, urgently. I had no fronts or walls up where he was concerned. Not anymore. So I had no reason to play coy, or try lying. Not only was I going to let him kiss me, I was going to let him do whatever the hell he wanted. He didn't even have to ask.

The new music was a slow song I didn't recognize, but we swayed back and forth like we were in middle school—Ty's hands never leaving my neck. It was pure bliss, and yet, it was some form of torture as well.

What was he waiting for?

Leaning in, I was about to take control, but he stopped me by pulling back on my neck. Looking into my eyes, he gave me a knowing smirk before crashing his lips to mine.

Finally.

It was only a few minutes, but the wait felt like years, and Ty knew what it was doing to me. What he didn't anticipate was what it did to him in return.

His attempt to keep control was lost as our kiss deepened and our dance slowed. He blindly backed me into the barre and lifted me so I sat on top of it. He held me in place by pressing his body between my open legs and his chest against mine.

It was late, and no one was coming in. I didn't check, but I had no doubt Ty locked the door when he entered. I never could have imagined myself stumbling so far that I had sex in my studio. The prima ballerina in me wanted to cringe, but the needy woman in me wanted to celebrate.

Pawing at Ty's clothes, I let him know it was time to lose them. If we were going to dance the way we were, and kiss the way we were, then he didn't need to waste time holding back.

Ty pulled up, leaving me sitting on the barre with my legs dangling. He lifted his hands to his back, showing me the tattoos on his triceps before pulling his shirt over his head and throwing it to the ground.

My eyes widened and Ty stood still, letting me soak him in. He was sculpted to perfection with dark-tanned skin and tattoos strategically placed all over his arms and torso. He had a small patch of hair that led below his loose-fitting shorts, and a very hard dick trying to find its way to me.

He kept his eyes on me as he toed off his shoes, followed by his socks. I bit my lip and jumped off the barre, getting close enough to run my fingers in every dip he had in his chest and stomach. He watched as my fingers moved back and forth, slowly making their way down to his shorts.

I hooked one finger in his elastic waistband and pulled, watching to see his reaction. He started biting his own lip, sucking air harshly between his teeth, waiting to see what I did.

"Take them down," he ground out.

Using my one hooked finger, I pulled down hard enough until his cock sprung free from the confines of his shorts. He had nothing else on under the shorts and I had never been happier with that knowledge.

I used my other hand to grab a hold of him and squeezed, wanting to see for myself if he felt as hard as he looked. I could see precum seeping from the head and I was so tempted to lean down and lick it off.

Ty didn't give me that chance, though. Squeezing him had

been like pressing a button and he went to another level instantly.

My shirt was being swept over my head and my leggings were being pulled down in a rush of unchecked fervor. I was spun around, facing the barre and the mirror, watching him stroke himself behind me.

All I had left on was my sports bra, panties, and ballet flats, and when I attempted to take them off, Ty swatted my thigh and shook his head.

"Leave the shoes on, Miss Priss."

I left them on, but took my bra and panties off before leaning forward and holding on to the barre. I was inviting him to me, urging him to enter me. Through the mirror, I wanted to watch, see his face, and know what he looked like when he was coming.

Scooting up behind me, with his shorts around his thighs, he took a finger through my center to test how wet I was. We groaned in unison when he did, but neither of us was surprised by how needy I was for him.

Once again, the music switched, and as if he had planned the steps, Ty lined up and pushed into me, the beat matching his rhythm as he got himself deeper. His hands found my breasts and he held tight, pinching my nipples to elicit a moan from me.

When he was buried as deep as he could go, he stopped moving, and I looked up into the mirror to watch his face. His eyes were closed and his head was turned to the side. I could tell he was doing everything in his power to keep himself in check.

"Don't hold back," I told him as I squeezed his cock inside of me.

His eyes opened and locked on mine in the mirror. If he thought I was taunting him, then so be it. Maybe I was. He may have thought I was "Miss Priss," but that was just what I let him see. It was completely different than what I was going to let him feel and I wanted to make sure he knew I could handle it.

Taking his hands from my breast, he stayed inside of me as he took the tie from my hair. My wavy strands fell loosely onto my shoulders and he gathered them up until they were securely in his left hand.

Then he pulled so hard my neck popped and I screamed in surprise. In the same motion, his right hand found my clit and he started pumping into me harder. He was hitting a spot in me that had never been reached, and I had the urge to place a hand on my lower stomach.

"Keep your hands on the barre," his voice was so husky and deep I barely recognized it, but I did as he said and refrained from pulling a hand off.

He pulled on my hair as he hit that deep spot over and over again, and before I could even prepare myself, or even try to hold it off, I exploded in an orgasm so fierce I thought I would fall. It took me several minutes to reorient myself, but Ty never stopped or let up, building another spiral of tension inside of me.

In the mirror, he was watching me, using my hair to control my head, pulling me to the side. The space allowed him to see us in the mirror, connected and rabid.

His face was exactly what I expected from someone like Ty—focused only on the sexual satisfaction we were getting from one another. He was zoned out, and for a minute, I wasn't even sure if he knew or cared who he had his dick inside.

The goal was pleasure, fulfillment, and distraction. I knew that before we started, and it was the main reason I let myself go so quickly. But I wanted him to know and remember who he was with at that moment.

Pushing back, I fought against his hold on my hair and lifted from the barre. I leaned my head back onto his shoulder, the way I did when we were dancing and held on to his neck with one arm. Turning my head, I found his lips, taking him by surprise and causing him to lose his grip on my hair.

It was an awkward position because of our height difference and he was having to hold me by my waist to keep from sliding out of my body. But I didn't care. His lips took me to another level and I started to grind on the air in front of me, seeking friction.

There weren't enough hands for the position we were in so Ty pulled out, turned me around, and lifted me up before settling me back down on his cock. As I wrapped my legs around his waist, our lips found each other again.

The new position was hitting somewhere else, somewhere deeper, and I felt that familiar tension growing in my stomach again.

"I'm gonna come," Ty warned with a scratchy voice.

It may have been a stupid decision because we both knew we weren't using protection, but I was so close and didn't want him to stop.

"Come inside me, Ty. Let me feel you," I pleaded.

He growled and grabbed a handful of my hair again, pumping himself into me fiercely. The moment I felt him let go was the moment my body started shaking, and my pussy started clenching involuntarily.

Ty kept moving, pushing until we were both spent and could no longer hold ourselves up. He lowered me to the ground and I fell back onto the wood floor, pulling his hand for him to do the same.

I was in nothing but my ballet flats and his shorts were still wrapped around his thighs. We lay side by side, hand in hand for two or three songs as the evidence of both of our orgasms slid down my leg and onto the floor.

Finally, Ty let out a small laugh, and I looked over at him. "What?"

"I just love the way we dance."

CHAPTER SEVENTEEN

"STEP, STEP, LEAP," Giselle was back in teacher mode and I was her little student.

After a few minutes of our post-sex glow, she had stood up and redressed, telling me we had to get to work. She was still frazzled and I could tell she had no regrets about what we had just done, but she was slowly creeping back into Miss Priss.

With the stress of what was going on with *Brise,* and the anxiety she felt for Sam, it didn't surprise me that she was trying to protect herself. But her uptight attitude only made me want to fuck her again.

In the meantime, I was a good boy and spent the evening doing leaps and steps. It felt like hours had passed as we lost track of time.

"Mr. Black," she clapped to get my attention, and I turned from my classical step to face her. "You are ready to combine a *plie, etendre, relever, glisser,* and *sauter.* We will then add an *elancer and tourner."*

"Do what?" I put my hands on my hips and snarled a bit to show my confusion.

Her lips tried quirking into a smile, but she suppressed it

quickly. "You will bend, stretch, rise, glide, and then jump. Once you do that, we will add a dart and a turn."

"Why the fuck didn't you just say that? Why does it have to be complicated?"

She couldn't suppress her smile that time and put her hands on her own hips. "At the risk of sounding redundant, I apologize."

"Fuck yeah, you do," I scoffed playfully.

"They are rather simple terms, though," she teased, and I fucking ate it up.

"Hac to tight right 42 power load Z reverse." I crossed my arms and raised one eyebrow, having just called out a football play that Cam may call in a huddle.

"What?"

"Psh, you should know," I whipped my hips around and snapped my fingers. "Its football baby. They are rather simple terms."

"Touché." She laughed, louder than I had ever heard from her before. It made me smile and my heart swell a little.

For the rest of the night, I did everything she told me to do, and I did it to the best of my ability. I didn't quite understand why the hell everyone thought some of it would help my game, but it made Giselle happy, and it seemed as though her smile was all I cared about.

When she finally called it a night, it was close to 10:30, and I was exhausted. In addition to dancing with Giselle, I had been practicing every day, and had barely been home. Knowing I had to get up early again the next morning and do it all over again was wearing on me.

Not to mention I hadn't seen my brother since seeing him outside of *Brise*. He wasn't answering his phone, but I knew he was still in town. It made me anxious and uneasy. The tension that had mounted in the past five minutes must have been evident because Giselle stared at me with concern on her face.

"Are you okay?"

"Just mentally making the decision to head out to the complex to sleep tonight," I shrugged. "It's a further drive, but I'm not really wanting to go home."

"Problems at home?" I could hear the curiosity oozing from that question. We hadn't really discussed the parameters of our personal lives before we fucked on that dance floor, and she was curious if I just cheated on someone I had at home. She wanted to know what kind of guy I was, and I couldn't blame her.

I was a good guy with a bad rap. One Google search didn't really give people the full picture of my story. Most of the issues I had were blamed on failed relationships and disgruntled women, but that was just the mask behind the real shit.

"My brother and his friends are staying there while they're in town," I started.

"Oh, do you two not get along?"

Fuck, our relationship was complicated. It wasn't about us not getting along, it was about us living in different worlds.

"We get along fine." It wasn't a lie because we did get along when shit was good. "We had fun all summer, and I don't want him to leave, but he likes to distract me from football."

"Do you think that is why you are struggling to focus?"

"Fuck yeah," I admitted. "I spend more time worried about him than I do worried about what foot I'm pushing off of."

"That's rough," she turned to gather her bag and I could see the pity she had for me on her face.

I didn't want her to think it was that big of an issue, so I countered one more time before ending the conversation. "He's my best friend. I would do anything for him, so I guess it makes sense that I worry about him. He's the only family I have, and we have each other's back. I'm just too tired to worry about him tonight, that's all."

As I finished speaking, I unlocked the door, taking a peak out before declaring it all clear. Giselle followed me and locked up, then headed toward the park across the street. It was a given that I was walking her home. She didn't ask, I didn't offer, we just knew that was how it went.

We both walked fairly silently, but I had taken her hand without thinking and intertwined our fingers. Her small smile was the only approval she gave me. There was no intention on my part to romanticize what we did together. Holding her hand was something I did before I ever had my dick inside of her. I wanted her to feel safe, and keeping my hold on her made me feel like I was doing that.

"I don't have any siblings. I bet it's fun."

"Only child?"

"Yep." The word *yep* sounded foreign on her lips, it was too slang for Miss Priss. I don't even think she realized I noticed those types of things.

"Parents?"

"Mom. She got pregnant with me while dancing in Russia and never even told my father I existed. By the time I was born, she had left Russia."

"She's a dancer?"

"You didn't know?"

"Seriously, Giselle, why would I know that?"

"My mother is Galena Metrovik. The ultimate prima ballerina. My grandparents helped raise me until I was nine, but then it was just her and me . She taught me everything I know. About dancing, presenting myself, and holding myself up."

That explained a lot. It told me exactly why she was so prim and proper. I nodded at myself, at my own realization that I had been right. She was born and bred on the other side of the tracks than I had been. She may not have had a father, but she had someone that cared about her presentation on the world.

I gave her a hard time for being uptight, but in reality, she was lucky to have someone who cared enough about her to teach her anything. The only thing my parents had taught me was how to disappear.

"She must love that you teach ballet."

"She would love it more if I had never left the stage. But I just needed to separate myself for a while. I was struggling."

Giselle bit her lip after her last word, almost as if she had said too much. I instinctively knew she didn't want me, or anyone else, to know she was struggling. She definitely didn't want me to know why. And since I had just battled the same thing inside of my own head, I didn't push.

"Looking forward to the game Sunday?"

"I almost blissfully forgot about that," she groaned.

"You know you're excited."

She looked back to me and smiled. "I'm looking forward to spending time with Sam."

"Oh," I snapped, reaching for the phone in my pocket. "Give me your number in case you have any issues."

She rattled off her number, and I texted her so she had mine. Her phone pinged in her bag, and I nodded to tell her it was me.

Once we reached her building, she turned to face me without letting my hand go, and smiled. Taking control, she leaned toward me, placing a kiss on my cheek. I should have been relieved that she chose that innocent gesture to say goodnight, but her lips touching my skin only lit me on fire again.

She started to walk away, and I should have let her since I didn't know what I was doing, but instead, I pulled her hand and forced her back in front of me.

With my free hand, I pulled on the back of her neck and crushed my lips to hers. Had I not been so wild with lust, I would have laughed at myself for being worried about kissing her in the first place. It was how every night should end. We weren't a love match and would never be, but that didn't mean we weren't *something*.

For as long as we needed each other, we should take advantage of whatever we were willing to give. We were both dealing with so much other bullshit, and intimacy was something we could give one another to help curb the circumstances that we dealt.

When I pulled back and saw the lust in her eyes and her lips pouted from our kiss, I was tempted to pull her back in for more. But then I would never leave.

As I started backing up, I let her hand go and she turned to head inside the glass door. Just like always, I waited, wanting to make sure she was safely in the elevator before leaving.

When she hit the call button, she looked back and something in her snapped when she saw me there waiting for her. She rushed back to the glass door and opened it.

"Your brother doesn't live here," she sighed.

It took me longer than it should have to get the gist, but once I did, I lunged and pushed her toward the open elevator. Our lips were tangled and her bag fell to the ground.

Unlike in the studio, she was losing control by the second and climbing me like a tree. Lifting her up, I wrapped her legs around my waist and pushed her into the wall. The elevator resembled the studio, with mirrors all around and a bar bolted half way up on the wall.

I wasn't sure if we were moving, if she had selected a floor, or if the doors had even shut. Only once the sound of the elevator signaled that we had reached our floor did I realize we'd actually moved.

Keeping her wrapped around me, I looked into the hallway for where I thought I should go. It was an upscale building so there weren't many door options since each apartment had a lot of square footage, but I still didn't know where I was going.

"Left," Giselle mumbled against my neck as she licked and sucked my skin. I grabbed her bag and ran to the left, finding a large double door that I assumed had to be hers.

She jumped down long enough to fish her keys out and

unlock the door, and then once again, we were lost, fumbling through the open space of her apartment and tearing each other's clothes off.

There was no pretense or small talk, no awkwardness or fronts. I didn't take the time to tell her how nice her place was, and she didn't give a shit if I was thirsty, or wanted coffee.

"Left," was all she said, again. I looked left once again, saw an open door that led to her bedroom, and rushed through. I threw her onto the bed and stripped myself quickly as she did the same.

Climbing on top of her, I didn't even bother with foreplay or sweetness. I was assuming she was wet, and shoving my dick deep inside her was how I was going to find out. Making sure I didn't come like a rookie was the only pause there was before I lifted her legs and started pounding into her harder than I had before.

She screamed and moaned, cussed and tossed her head back and forth. She clawed at my shoulders and urged me to keep moving as hard as I could.

Sweat was dripping down my face and had formed between her breasts. It was so quick and passionate. We didn't give a shit what we looked like, or how we were presenting ourselves. We just wanted to chase an orgasm together.

When she finally stopped moaning and got quiet, I knew she was close, so I thumbed her clit and pushed her over.

"Ty, Ty, Ty," she chanted and I reveled in my name on her lips. I wasn't *Mr. Black* when she was coming.

Following her over the edge, I slowed down and unloaded inside of her, trusting that since I had done so earlier, we were okay to do it again. My knees buckled, my legs constricted, and I made a sound that I wasn't sure I had ever made before.

Giselle was spent, limp, and staring at where we were connected as I pulled out and fell next to her. We didn't speak, or talk things out, there was no need. I expected Miss Priss to return and for her to freak out for getting her blanket dirty, but she didn't even budge.

Her head fell to the side, her long hair fanning over the blanket, and she fell asleep next to me with a sated and satisfied look on her face. I knew I shouldn't have stayed, but I couldn't have moved if I tried, so I remained where I was and fell asleep as well.

giselle

"FUCK."

"Shit."

"Ouch."

Those were just a few of the whispered words I woke up to. I looked up to find Ty pacing around my room, looking for the clothes we had discarded the night before.

He hadn't realized I was awake and I smiled as I watched him jump on one foot from one side of the room to the other. He had his shorts back on but not his shirt and I could see the tattoos lining his body in the early morning light that had started streaming in.

I giggled when he made his way back into my eye line, hopping on the opposite foot as before, still no shirt. The noise caught his attention and he froze, looking at me.

The smile that formed on his face was breathtaking and I almost audibly gasped at how much he was affecting me. In all fairness, I wasn't sure I had ever seen him smile so brightly, and so genuinely, but a part of me wondered if maybe I was just extra smitten.

"Morning," he said as he sauntered toward the bed. I was still naked, but a blanket covered me, and my face was burrowed into a pillow.

"Morning," I lifted my mouth from the pillow and dropped it back down after I spoke.

He sat on the bed beside me and brushed the rogue strands of hair from my face. It was an extremely intimate motion that had goosebumps forming on my skin.

"I have to go to practice," Ty explained and I nodded, relieved that it kept things less awkward that morning. "You have my number, and I will text you what to do on Sunday for the game."

"Ok," I whispered with a smile in my tone.

"You okay?" He asked, but had a matching smile on his face.

"Oh yeah," I nodded and his smile got bigger.

"Good," he kissed my temple and stood up, throwing his shirt over his head. "See you Sunday, Miss Priss."

He winked and was on his way out of my room when the doorbell rang. I sat up straight and covered my chest with the blanket as Ty froze and looked back at me. No one ever rang my doorbell.

Ever.

I didn't know anyone in Atlanta well enough for them to know where I lived—or to even need to know.

"I can get that," Ty said when he saw my eyes wide open with concern.

"I don't even know who it could be."

"Get dressed and I'll check."

I nodded and climbed from the bed. We both knew I was mostly worried because of what was going on at *Brise*. No way could that guy know where I lived, but what if he watched me, or followed me home one night?

I took a deep breath, knowing that scenario was unlikely, and also thankful that Ty was there. If someone was going to have the guts to come to my home, I was glad I wasn't alone.

I threw clothes on quickly and followed Ty into the living

room. He didn't pay much attention to his surroundings when we came in the night before, so I whispered to get his attention when he walked the wrong way to the door.

"That way," I pointed to the right.

Ty did an about-face and walked quickly into the foyer. He approached the door and instead of opening it, he wisely looked through the peephole.

"Who is it?" I whispered, creeping closer.

Instead of answering, Ty stumbled backward almost tripping on his own feet. He propelled as fast as he could without looking where he was going and fell over the back of my white couch.

If he was that shaken up, I was downright terrified. I started to scream and grab my phone to call 911.

"Who is it? Is it a bad guy? Do they have a gun?"

Ty was on the floor, peeking over the back of the couch as if he was in a foxhole. He was shaking his head *no* at all my questions and I started jumping with anxiety.

"Worse," Ty finally muttered.

What could be worse? Terrorist? Someone from the census committee?

Or… "Oh my God, is it a salesman?"

"It's my coach."

Instinct had me on the verge of screaming so it took me a minute to register what he had said.

"Wait, what?" I stood up straight and looked back and forth from him to the door.

"Shhhh, its my coach. If we're quiet, he'll go away."

"Oh my God, Ty," I squealed with relief. I started making my way to the door to open it. There was a directory for the building so there was no doubt how Mr. Peyton found out which apartment I lived in. I just wasn't sure what would have him knocking on my door so early. Especially without calling or texting me first.

I started toward the door, not worried about Ty, more

concerned about what brought Mr. Peyton to my home. But before I made it to the door, Ty threw me over his shoulder and took me right back to the couch, ducking behind it.

"What the hell is your problem?" I swatted at him.

"It's Coach," he said slowly, like that explained everything.

"So?" I stared at him with one eye squinted and my nose scrunched up.

"So?" Ty started waving his hands. "He can't know I fucked my ballet teacher. Do you have any idea what he'll do to me if he knows about this?"

I giggled a little because even with my mom being who she was, I was never worried about her judging me for who I had sex with.

"You don't get it. Coach is the closest thing to a father I have ever had. He signed me up for fucking ballet lessons, for fucks sake. He cares about my wellbeing, and has a plan in place for me. Fucking the teacher is going against his plans."

Ok, I could understand that but, "What is he going to think when I show up at the game Sunday?"

"He will think I gave you and your student my tickets. He probably won't even see you."

"I need to see what he wants," I started to stand up but Ty pulled me back down into hiding.

"No, you don't."

"You do realize he cannot see us through that door, right?"

Ty was shaking his head in disbelief and pursing his lips, "He probably can."

"How does a guy with tattoos and muscles all over his body fear another person this much?"

"I don't fear for my safety, Miss Priss, I fear for my football career."

I rolled my eyes and gave up, falling next to him to hide. It was the second time he and I had been on the floor, hiding from another person, and I was wondering if it was our thing. Something we would always find ourselves doing.

After a few more minutes, Ty started to peek over the couch, as if he could see through the walls. He looked around and must have declared the coast clear because he got up and walked toward the door again.

Peeking through the hole, I could hear the audible sigh of relief he released so I assumed Mr. Peyton was gone.

"We can't do this again," Ty leaned against the door and tilted his head back.

Even though I shouldn't have cared, I was kind of offended. Was I that easy to walk away from? Sex with Ty was not going to be easy to forget and I was kind of hoping we would keep that up for a while. Being dismissed made me feel like I wasn't near as memorable for him.

Of course, for a guy like Tyson Black, I was probably mediocre. It wasn't like I had a ton of experience and he was probably used to being with women that did all kinds of tricks and stunts. My pride was a little hurt, but I wasn't going to let Ty see me pout about it. I definitely didn't need to give him fuel for driving me crazy.

"Next time needs to be at my place. Coach would never show up there," Ty continued his thought.

His words popped me out of my self-pity party and I looked up at him. He was still against the door and was barely looking at me, so I was sure he didn't say that just to appease me.

After the internal pep talk I had just given myself, I should have been strong enough to say, *"Nah, let's just call it quits."* But I didn't, because I didn't want to.

So instead I asked, "What about your brother?"

"He doesn't care who I have sex with," Ty scoffed and pushed himself from the door. He made his way to me and once again leaned down to kiss my cheek. "I gotta go beat Coach to the complex."

"Have fun," I mumbled as I watched him leave.

I stood still, exactly where I had been when Ty left, for way longer than necessary. I was just so dumbfounded over everything that had transpired that morning. Ty was definitely not boring.

Once I got a handle on everything, I threw myself into the shower and tore the dirty sheets from my bed. I didn't have to be at *Brise* because there were no classes, and since I was up, I settled on chores to get me through the morning.

Later, I needed to do a few things to get prepared for the following week, like getting the police department to leave an officer outside the door of *Brise*. I knew it wasn't feasible for every business but I was hoping my plea for the safety of the kids would spur them to make someone available.

If not, I was prepared to hire an off-duty officer. There was just no way I could cancel classes forever, but I wasn't going to be okay with that choice until I knew we had a safety net.

The time I spent there with Ty didn't bother me, even though that was the time I was most likely to get an unwanted visitor. Ty had no business being put in danger either, but I couldn't ask an officer to stand outside while I most likely had sex.

I rolled my eyes at myself as my phone dinged with a message. I expcted it to be a parent or my mom, but Mr .Peyton's name appeared as I unlocked my phone.

> I stopped by this morning to invite you to the game on Sunday. It was early, and I know just stopping by is rude, but I thought you would have a harder time saying no in person and it was the only time I had.

I panicked, trying to think of something to say.

> I must have been asleep.

Did I tell him I was already coming to the game? I didn't know what to do. Ty said the tickets weren't a big deal so he didn't care about me telling Mr. Peyton, right? While I was busy trying to decide, my phone dinged again.

> Tyson was limping at practice this morning but insisted he was fine. Did things go ok last night?

Yeah they were pretty good. Not sure why he was the one limping since it was my legs that were pressed to my face, but whatever. None of that was shit I could reply with.

> Yes sir. He did start a slide and jump combination so maybe he is sore.

> Ah maybe. He definitely won't admit it if that's the case.

> Can I talk you into coming Sunday?

> Actually, Mr. Black offered tickets to me and a student of mine, and his mom.

> He did what???????

Oh shit! Maybe it was a big deal. I hoped I didn't get him in trouble.

> I can cancel, it is no problem.

> No, no! Please come! Ty has never shared his tickets with anyone though, so I am just surprised. That's all.

That left me with so many questions and none of the answers were any of my business.

CHAPTER NINETEEN

I PRESSED CALL when I got in my car and waited for the bluetooth to connect to my phone. When I heard her voice come over the speaker, I smiled.

"Hello?" It was definitely a question, as if she knew who was calling, just wasn't sure why.

"Hey Miss Priss, how are ya?"

"Is this a booty call?"

I almost swerved off the road, taken by surprise at her direct words.

"Um, no?" I was asking my own questions. Was it a booty call? I didn't intend for it to be, but if she told me to come over, I would. Even though I said I couldn't go over there anymore, I was lying through my teeth—even to myself. At the time, I had just been running on adrenaline.

"Then how can I help you, Mr. Black?"

"Are you back to that already? I literally had my dick inside of you not even 24 hours ago. It amazes me how quickly you can swap personalities."

"I've been working all day," she said by way of explanation. I got what she was doing, and why she presented herself the way she did. I just didn't want to be on the receiving end of it anymore. I wanted wild Giselle. I wanted access to the Giselle who rolled her eyes and hid behind couches with me.

"I think I bruised my ankle leaping over your couch this morning."

"That actually explains a lot and leads to more questions all at the same time."

"Yeah? How so?"

"Mr. Peyton texted me and said you were limping. Of course he wondered if it had happened in class. Not to worry, I didn't tell him about your fall."

"I didn't fall, it was more of a *sauter.*"

"As impressed as I am with your use of ballet terminology, you most definitely fell. Like…sacked."

"Sacked?" I laughed.

"That is 'football' for backward," she declared.

I didn't correct her, she wasn't completely wrong. Giselle was getting pretty irresistible. She tried so hard to put on a façade, but when it slipped, it was like hitting the promise land.

That was why I called her. I knew I wouldn't see her until Sunday, and I fucking missed her. I wanted to hear her say something uppity so I could knock her back down with some vapid commentary. It was my new favorite thing to do.

"You looking forward to the game Sunday?" I smirked at myself, knowing she wasn't.

"Yes, Mr. Peyton offered me better tickets than you did, so I'm looking forward to that."

I stiffened and pressed my foot on the pedal a little harder. Was I going to have to kick Coach's ass? Shit I didn't want to, but I would. He would probably put up a serious fight because Coach was no slouch, but when it came to him trying to trump me with Giselle, I would have the upper-hand.

Fuck.

Now I was not only calling her on a Friday night, but I was

mentally kicking my coach's ass for her. What the hell was wrong with me? Was the sex that good?

"Fuck yeah it was," my dick said quietly.

It was more than that, though. I actually liked Giselle, even her pretentious side. Maybe even *because* of her pretentious side.

"Okay that's cool," I finally said, my voice catching unconvincingly.

Giselle must have heard it too because she started laughing uncontrollably.

"Just joking. He invited me but I told him you had already given me tickets."

Not sure that was any better, but I knew him finding out was a possibility, so I had to be okay with that.

"Cool," I played it off, though not very well. *Cool* seemed to be the only word I could squeak out.

"He said you never gave those tickets away before. Should Sam and I feel special?"

Knowing she couldn't see me, I shook my head because the reason behind that was not very exciting. It wasn't like I coveted those tickets. I just never had anyone in my life worth a shit to give them to. Not even my brother wanted to come to any of my games. He and his friends were too busy causing havoc everywhere they went, so even if they wanted to, I wouldn't have invited them just based on that fact.

"Yeah, you guys are special," I ended up telling her since it was the truth.

"Why did you call, Ty?" I loved it when she called me Ty. How did just the two letters of my name become so deep, so fast?

"I missed you," I said with more honesty.

"So this *is* a booty call?"

"No Miss Priss, I'm halfway home, and need to deal with my brother before tomorrow. I think I really did just miss you."

She processed my words with a few quiet breaths before responding. "Unbelievably enough, I miss you too."

My smile could have lit my way home with how bright it was. In that instant, I knew I was getting a little too attached to Giselle, but I couldn't bring myself to find a downside to that as long as Coach didn't find out—at least not until he wasn't paying her for my lessons anymore.

"Tell Mrs. Watson to meet you at gate D. There is a Family and Friends Will Call booth there. Just give them my name, have an ID ready, and they'll give you my tickets."

"Okay, I can do that," she drifted off and I knew she was writing everything down. It would be like her to take specific and hardcore notes on the process of attending a football game. "Anything else?"

"Yep," I had just decided then and there on something else. "I'll instruct Will Call to give you a pass for the post-game waiting area. It's right outside the locker room. Show the pass to the staff after the game and they'll escort you to the right spot."

At least I hoped that was how it worked, I hadn't really ever done that, but Giselle was going to need a plan if I expected her to follow through and wait for me.

"Sam will enjoy that," she was still writing all it down as she listened. "Anything else?"

I knew Sam would enjoy that, but I was going to enjoy it more. I ended every game with an adrenaline rush, pent up energy, and nowhere to deposit it all. If I couldn't shake it off before getting home, I would sometimes end up working out after a game.

But now, Giselle was going to be where it all went. She just had no idea yet. I was not a man of many surprises, though, so before hanging up, I warned her.

"Yeah," my tone was husky and deep, taking on meaning all on its own. "Don't wear any panties, Miss Priss. And wear your hair up in that tight bun… I want to be the one that unravels it."

With my final comment, I hung up on Giselle, not giving her a chance to tell me no. When I saw her sitting in the stands and watching the game on Sunday, I would know by her hair if she was on board.

The thought of her cheering for me with her hair twisted up tight and no panties on was making me hard again. She was going to be the death of me if I couldn't get myself together.

Whipping my car into my parking spot at my apartment, I looked around to see if I saw my brother's SUV. It was there, sitting in the corner of the parking garage. I had a feeling he would be there, and I needed to talk to him once and for all about his trip to *Brise*—and the stare-down he gave me on the sidewalk.

He was leaning against the bar in the kitchen with his arms crossed, staring at the floor, when I walked in. It wasn't what I expected so I stopped and tilted my head, wondering if he even heard or saw me come in.

"I found a place," he huffed without looking at me.

"Good, bro. If you're staying in Atlanta, you need your own place."

I inched further into the kitchen and leaned on the counter across from him, crossing my arms and mimicking his stance. The only difference was, I was looking at him, wondering why he was being so dramatic.

"Marcus and Devon got into some shit I'm not comfortable with and I told them to get the fuck out of town," he was shaking his head and looking sad. "They were going to room with me so it looks like it's just me."

Was that the part where I was supposed to say something about him not moving out? That if it is just him then he could stay? Because that wasn't going to happen. I didn't realize Mike had morals that Marcus and Dev didn't, but that didn't change the fact that he and I were not a good fit. Especially when it came to football season.

"Sorry to hear that, man."

Before I could ask, he looked up and asked me first. "What were you doing at *Brise*?"

"I was going to ask you the same thing."

"I asked first."

"The owner is a friend of mine."

"Monday morning is a strange time to visit," he pushed.

"I could say the same for you."

He raised his hands up in surrender and shook his head, "Can I be honest?"

My eyes opened wide and I lifted one side of my mouth, almost wanting to laugh. "Please."

"I got a major boner for the chick there," he bit his lip and made a noise I wanted to hit him for. There was no way in hell I was going to let him think about, or touch anything when it came to Giselle.

"How do you know her?" I asked, intentionally not using her name.

"I don't," he scoffed. "I was going to go in and talk to her, fake having a kid that needed lessons or something."

"Yet you ended up in the nail salon," I deadpanned.

He laughed and stood up straight, "I saw a friend of mine through the window. I went and told her I had a boner and needed her help. Poor thing didn't realize the boner was for the dance lady. I waited outside until she was done with her appointment, and that's when I saw you walking into *Brise* with my girl."

He sounded a bit angry, like I had infringed upon his territory. I didn't like the way he called Giselle his girl, but I refrained from telling him it was *my* dick she was riding. Maybe if he hadn't disappeared all week, we could have talked about it before, and I would have left her alone for his sake.

Probably not, but maybe.

One thing I knew for sure was that Giselle wouldn't give my brother the time of day. She was way too good for him. She was too good for me, which was why it would never be more than sex.

But Mike? He was trouble on another level, and Giselle would see through that. She wasn't the type of person to swoon over lies and words like "boner." She would see Mike come in with his loose-fitting clothes and patchy goatee and tell him to get lost.

On the other side, though. If Mike saw Giselle and was crushing, I wasn't sure what it would do to the little bit of brotherly love we had left if I told him she was mine.

"I met her through Coach and helped her for a minute that morning," I finally blurted.

"So that's it?"

"That's it," I lied.

"Sorry I avoided you all week, bro." Mike pulled me into a hug and patted my back. "You're all I have left, and I just don't want there to be any shit between us. I know you need your space. I know you gotta do football and shit. I know I haven't always been the best support for that. I know why you asked me to leave." He leaned back and kept his hands on my shoulders, looking me in the eye. "I was hurt when I saw you walk in with my girl, but you didn't know I was crushing so I shouldn't have been avoiding you. We okay?"

I nodded and rolled my eyes. I had said it a million times—to myself, to Coach—Mike was not a bad brother. He would never hurt me, intentionally. He knew we didn't see eye to eye and he accepted that time and time again. He would probably be excited if I went to work with him, but he knew football was where my heart was.

"I got my place," Mike backed away and grabbed some keys off the bar. "I wanted to see you and chat this out, but I'm going home." He winked at me when he said the word home and started toward the door.

Without considering how much I really shouldn't ask, I was curious about one thing. "What did Marc and Dev do?"

Mike turned around and shook his head, "You don't want to know, Lil Bro, trust me. Just know I wasn't putting up with their shit, and they're out."

"Okay," I nodded. He was right, I didn't want to know, but, "You going to keep pursuing Giselle?"

I said her name without thinking, but I knew he would have found out somehow if he really wanted to.

"Nah," he frowned and shook his head, smiling a little at me. "I got the hots for her, but not as much as you do." He winked again and opened the door, yelling, "Love you bro," as he left.

The door clicked shut and I had to think about what he had just implied. He knew, he fucking knew. Without a doubt. I assumed he could tell by the way I looked and the way I said her name. I stupidly asked if he was going after her and that was all it took for him to know I was interested.

And yet, he said he would back off—for me.

I wasn't going to admit anything to him, ever. He probably knew neither of us was good enough for her, but if thinking I stood a chance, or cared, kept him away from her, then I accepted that.

Grabbing my phone, I walked to the door and locked it, then headed to the bedroom. I had already showered at the complex after practice, so I flopped into my bed and relished the quiet.

Then I grabbed my phone and shot one more text to Miss Priss.

What are you wearing?

giselle

"WHAT ARE YOU WEARING?"

Ty's text made me laugh out loud to myself, and I answered with a quick, *"Sweatpants and a facemask."*

Once he shot back with, *"So hot,"* I didn't answer him back and he didn't send anymore. If I had known he wasn't going to call Saturday, and I wouldn't talk to him again until after the game Sunday, I probably would have bantered with him a little more.

As it turned out, I kind of missed him. He had a way about him that made me relax and smile more than I had in a long time. He made me feel like my entire life didn't have to be a show. I wanted more of it and was scared of it all at the same time.

Tyson Black and I were not a love match, but there was no doubt that our bodies enjoyed one another. That was why my hair was up tight in a bun and I had no panties on under my jeans as I made my way into the football stadium on Sunday.

Wondering what Ty would think made me smile to myself. He would know by looking at me what I had in mind, and a small thrill for the game made its way down my spine.

I had met Sam and Mrs. Watson at the gate and we took our seats in the front row on the fifty yard line. The seats were like first class recliners, with TVs in front of every seat and a waitress walking around asking if we needed anything.

Ty had told us these seats were for player friends and families, VIPs, and anyone of that nature. When they put the stadium together, they put a lot of thought into that area and I was in awe.

As if that wasn't enough, it was my first time seeing a football game in person, and the hype around the entire stadium was exhilarating. Almost more so than being on stage.

The fans were louder, crazier, wilder. And the fact that it was a preseason game had me especially in shock. What was the real season like?

After sitting down, Sam and I had fallen into a normal conversation discussing school, friends, and all his favorite things. I kept myself in check and didn't dare start pressing on him about dancing. Ty had set our day up as a time to connect with Sam and that was all I really wanted to do. I knew it wasn't the same as having friends his own age, but I wanted him to know he had at least one friend who supported his love of dancing.

Thirty minutes before the game was scheduled to start, I got a text on my phone that I intended to ignore. But after a follow-up text, I let it interrupt our conversation in case something was terribly wrong.

> About to head out and warm up.
>
> I'm #82.
>
> Are you wearing panties?
>
> If I end up in the end zone, watch the way I dance.

I smiled at Ty's messages and stuffed the phone back into my bag, not even answering. The grin on my face must have been sillier than I anticipated, though, because Sam was looking at me with a weird expression.

"Oh um," I played with my fingers as I spoke to Sam. "That was Mr. Black. He wanted to let me know he was headed out soon."

Sam yelled and jumped for joy, not paying attention to my loss of poise. He stood between his mother and me, clapping, looking in all the different directions for the Jets to come out.

It wasn't long before the lights dimmed and the announcer started his introductions. Fire flew from cannons, and considering we were in a dome, it was quite impressive. I got goosebumps as I looked up at the screen and saw several different videos of the players.

The crowd started screaming and I looked around for what had set them off. Sam started pointing to our left and I caught sight of the team exiting the tunnel just as his little screams peaked. He was definitely a fan and the environment was hyping him up in a way ballet never could.

As the team made their way onto the field, they lined up on the yard lines much like they did when I went to their practice. They started moving in sync, stretching and flexing at the same time in the same way. A coach was on the side of the field counting, and making sure they all stayed on task.

Scouring the lines of players, I searched for #82. My eyes went up and down the lines, back and forth, until finally, I saw him. He was stretched into a lunge and bouncing before switching legs. His hands were on his hips to keep his balance and his helmet was on his head.

I wasn't very close, but from the first row I was sitting in, I could see his forearms flexing and his calf muscles straining. He was in all white—jersey, pants, and cleats—and it made the dark ink of his tattoos stand out even more.

While everyone else in that stadium was excited to see the team play, I was excited for after the game, when I got to take #82 back to my place and make him do things to me that he wasn't yet aware I would allow.

"I see Ty!" Sam yelled, popping me out of my lust-filled thoughts.

"I see him!" I clapped excitedly with Sam and watched as he explained all the other players to me.

"That's Cam Nichols," he pointed to an extremely good-looking guy with his helmet off, passing the ball back and forth with someone else. "He's the quarterback. Best ever."

"I see. What about him?" I pointed to another guy that had the number 33 on his back.

"That's Damien Wilson, a running back. He's good, but honestly, he's only as good as his offensive line."

"And who is that?"

"The offensive line?"

"Yeah, which number is he?"

Sam looked at me like I was crazy for a second but then gently explained. "The offensive line is made up of the five guys that line up in front of the quarterback. They kinda have to be good to allow the offense time to do their thing." I was nodding, trying to understand but Sam sighed heavily and added. "Just watch, you'll see."

As Sam finished telling me about the head coach—Mr. Peyton, as I liked to call him—the team made their way from their lines and to the side of the field closest to our seats.

Looking on, I saw Ty take his helmet off as he jogged in our direction. He looked up and smiled when he saw us, sending us all three a small wave. Then he took a minute to twirl his hand on top of his head and give me a thumbs up. Knowing he was pointing out my hair, I turned bright red, and had to remind myself that it was our little secret.

Ty winked at me when he saw me flush, but quickly turned around to his team and got down to business. The game started moments later, and in no time, I found my voice yelling at the top of my lungs. Sam and I high-fived every good play and if I wasn't sure if it was a good play, he patiently held his hands up until I caught on and high-fived him.

Mrs. Watson was equally enthusiastic, and I thought for a moment that it was the first time I had ever seen her that happy. The thrill had gotten to her too; and with the luxury around us and the special way we were treated, I bet she was having the time of her life.

My heart warmed to Ty's intentions, thinking of how I would have missed the joy on Sam's face had he not strong-armed me into going to the game. I also would have missed the look on Ty's face when he came back from half time.

His smirk was bold as he eyed me in the crowd. He pointed two fingers at his eyes and then pointed toward the goal before taking his place on the field for the first play of the second half.

Cam Nichols ran backward a few steps and then threw the ball to Ty. The first thing I noticed was the development of his sprint, starting with the toe of his shoes and keeping his feet in the right direction. Then I noticed the leap he made, clearing over another player from the other team and catching the ball in the air.

Instead of landing and falling to the ground, he turned slightly and allowed his other foot to do some work. It was a perfect jeté and my heart soared with pride as I watched him stick the landing. Afterward, he righted himself and ran down the field to score a touchdown.

If there was any doubt what was going on, it was made clear by Sam jumping up and down, pulling on my arm, and yelling, "Touchdown, Ty. Touchdown, Ty."

I kept my eyes on Ty and watched as he celebrated with his teammates. They were all tapping his helmet and crowding him with joy. But once they cleared, Ty started a quick classical walk, added a less than stellar *pas de chat,* and then turned toward the crowd to do a Harlem ballroom vogue.

My jaw was dropped so far open a football could have fit in my mouth. His ballet steps looked awful, and chances were, unless you were the one watching him two nights a week do the same thing, you wouldn't have a clue what he was doing.

"He always does a touchdown dance like that," Sam said, mimicking his vogue. "Not sure what that other stuff was, though."

I had to bite my lip to keep from laughing because Sam said exactly what I was thinking. As smart and talented as Sam was in the art of ballet, even he couldn't tell what Ty was doing.

"That was interesting," I tilted my head and pursed my lips. "A little weird, but looked fun."

I came very close to telling Sam that Ty was mimicking our dance lessons, but Ty still didn't want anyone to know and that meant Sam as well.

We all continued to have a great time, but at the end of the third quarter, Mrs. Watson's cell phone rang.

"Hello?" She answered. *"What?"* Her brows furrowed and she looked at Sam. "We'll head that way right now. Piedmont?"

Mrs. Watson stood as she hung up and started gathering her things.

"What happened?" I asked.

Mrs. Watson paused and looked at me, I could see tears glistening in her eyes. She looked to Sam and then back to me, debating on how much she wanted to say in his presence.

"My oldest son's been shot," she hiccupped and swallowed her tears.

"Oh my God!" I stood up frantically, feeling like there was something I should do.

"Reggie?" Sam cried at the same time.

"It's... it's ok." She took a deep breath and pushed the air down with her hands to compose herself. "They said it was a flesh wound and he will be fine, but I need to get to the hospital."

"Can I do anything? Do you want me to get Sam home?"

"No, I wanna go, momma," Sam cried.

"Oh, sweet Miss Metro, we appreciate this so much. We have had a wonderful time, but I want to keep Sam with me. I cannot imagine being away from one of my babies right now."

"Of course," I nodded, patting my legs, looking around for something to grab, some way to help.

"You just tell Mr. Black thank you for us," she added. "This was an experience we will never forget."

"I will tell him as soon as the game is over."

Guilt raced through me and I started shaking visibly. It wasn't my son, it wasn't my issue, so I should have been the one consoling Mrs. Watson. Instead, she noticed my worry and pulled me into a big hug.

"Don't worry, Miss Metro. This may be just the blessing we were praying for. Reggie has been running with the wrong crowds, and at this point, I'm just thankful they didn't call to tell me he was dead."

We both took a deep breath at her words and separated. There seemed to be so much trouble in Atlanta. I had yet to tell the parents about my own run in with the *wrong crowd* and a part of me knew that was why I was shaking so much.

Why was good news so hard to find?

I tapped the top of Sam's head and gave him a sad smile, "Hope to see you in class, Tuesday."

"I can't wait," Sam sounded happy despite the news of his brother and I was taking that small sign as a win for the day. I just wanted Sam to be happy.

They left quickly and I sat back down, alone. Looking around to take stock of the game, I found Ty standing with his back to me and his helmet in his hand. His ass looked so good in his tight football pants that for a minute, I thought about demanding he wear tights in the studio from there on out.

He would probably laugh at me and give me shit, so I was definitely going to. I loved when he gave me shit. I loved giving it right back to him. I couldn't wait until the game was over and I could tell him everything he did wrong during his touchdown dance.

The last quarter flew by without Ty seeing much playing time. That meant he was standing in the same position for a solid thirty minutes, and if it weren't for the fireworks, I wouldn't have realized the game was over.

I took the pass Ty had left me and hung it around my neck, making my way up the steps to the lobby of the section we were in. He had told me there was an elevator I could take that opened up directly into the waiting area, so I headed to the only one I saw close by.

Flashing my pass for good measure, I followed a few others into the elevator and let the operator hit the buttons to take us down.

There was a couple standing in the opposite corner and I overheard the woman say, "I cannot wait to kiss Cam's face. I hate watching him get hit all night." Which seemed odd because her arms were wrapped around the other guy like they were the ones that did the kissing.

I assumed the *Cam* she was speaking of was the quarterback since they were headed in the same direction as me. That thought was confirmed with the man's following statement and it peaked my intrigue even more.

"Go easy on him baby, he took a few hits tonight," the guy said to her and kissed the top of her head.

"Jets need a better left guard," she huffed, causing the man to laugh.

The doors to the elevator opened, and the man motioned for me to go out first. I didn't really know where I was going but thankfully, as I exited, there was a sign that led me to the right and a bunch of people waiting around, chatting.

The couple followed me out and was instantly surrounded by

others when they entered the room. Meanwhile, I stood alone, trying to look like I knew what I was doing.

Every so often, someone would come out of the double doors to our left and shake a few hands before exiting the glass doors to our right. The men coming from the double doors were huge, with major muscles and expensive clothes. It didn't take a rocket scientist to realize they were players.

Feeling a bit off-kilter, I grabbed my phone and started fumbling through random things. As I did so, a quick thought popped into my head.

GOOGLE: Cam Nichols' Girlfriend

Sure enough, the woman I saw in the elevator was pictured with Cam and the other guy I saw, whose name was Kace Jackson. I read further and found out he was a baseball player in Atlanta. It wasn't confirmed, but the headlines indicated she was in a relationship with both of them.

"Holy shit," I mumbled.

"Right?" I heard over my shoulder.

At the risk of being embarrassed, I jumped and my phone went flying from my hands onto the floor. Ty was laughing and chasing my phone as I stood there with my hands over my mouth to hide my scream.

"Damn, Miss Priss," Ty said as he handed me my phone. "Did I scare you?"

I was nodding with what I was sure was a horrified expression. He clearly saw what I was looking at.

Ty took pity on me and pulled me into a hug. "Don't worry, we have all Googled that shit. They are interesting, for sure."

His words instantly eased a little bit of the tension I felt, and I rubbed my face into his shirt. He smelled clean, freshly showered and a hint of something fragrant—black leather, Cardamom, Patchouli? Whatever it was, it appealed to me on another level, and I inhaled as I continued to hide my face.

"I rode down in the elevator with them and got curious," I admitted.

"You aren't the only one, I promise."

I looked up and smiled at him, still holding onto his shirt. At that moment, I felt like we were a couple. Like I had just watched my man play and was meeting him after the game. In a sense, that was exactly what it was, but if I wanted to dissect it further, it was really just a means to sex for us.

Still, as if we were a real couple, Ty leaned in and kissed my nose before pulling away and taking my hand. He started leading me to the glass doors that everyone else was leaving through, but we were stopped a few times.

"Who is this?" A woman with red hair and porcelain skin asked.

"This is Giselle. Giselle? This is Amanda."

She surveyed me up and down as she shook my hand. "What are you two?"

I started to say that we were just friends, but Ty beat me to it, "This is my girl."

Amanda's eyebrows raised up and she smirked at Ty, "Wow."

Who was this girl? An ex?

Ty just rolled his eyes at her and said a quick goodbye. I wish I could say that was the only time that happened but there were two similar encounters with two other people before we finally made it to the glass doors.

We walked through a small group of fans that were held back by barriers and then found silence when we entered the parking garage.

"Told ya," Ty said to me as we walked hand in hand.

"Told me what?"

"People are curious. At least you Googled your curiosity in private. Imagine being forward enough to ask someone to their face what their relationship status was."

"Are those your ex's or something?"

"None of them. The redhead is the owner's daughter. The other two were just family of other players. They were just curious."

"I can understand that," I laughed, finally feeling the tension fall completely away. Ty's reassurances were helping, but being alone with him was the main factor. "Where're we going?"

"Your hair is up in that tight bun and I'm willing to bet you have no panties on. Where do you think we're going?"

"My place?"

"No, my place." We reached his car, a shiny black sports car that looked like it cost more than my entire studio.

"Don't you have unwanted roommates?" I didn't want to be around other people. I didn't want to be a spectacle for Ty to parade around in front of his brother and friends. We could have all the sex we wanted to, but it didn't need to be for someone else's entertainment.

"They moved out Friday. Plus, I don't live far, and there is zero chance of Coach knocking on my door."

If we were going to be alone, I could handle going to Ty's, so I climbed into the passenger seat. When he got in on the other side, he slid his hand to my knee. It felt as though he did it without realizing he was doing it, like it just came naturally.

I spent the entire ride giving him the rundown on why Sam hadn't come to the waiting area with me. I explained about his brother and Ty tightened his grip on my leg as I spoke.

Shaking his head and tapping the steering wheel, he looked pissed and tempted to turn the car around and head to Piedmont. There wasn't anything we could do, and it really wasn't our place, so he refrained and pulled into the garage of his apartment building.

He didn't live directly downtown the way I did. The area was posher and up and coming on the outskirts of the city center. For some reason, I expected an overly ostentatious penthouse style bachelor pad that required a special code to even open the elevator.

To my surprise, Ty's apartment was an understated luxury. The building was well kept with quaint businesses and restaurants all around. We took the elevator to the modest sixth floor, where doors lined a long hallway.

Ty fumbled with a few keys but got the door open and led me into the entrance. I stopped and took stock of his place with its leather couches and huge TV. There was a small dining area and a nicely equipped kitchen to the side.

"Come 'ere," Ty whispered as he pulled me in closer. Our kiss didn't start out sweet and unassuming. It was fierce and straight to the point.

"Fuck I've wanted to kiss you since Thursday," he groaned into my lips. "I want to keep kissing you. All. Fucking. Night."

I nodded as our lips stayed connected and went to lift his shirt slightly. He wasn't much help, in fact, he stopped me completely, causing me to pull my mouth from his.

"Fuck I have to eat," he moaned like it was a chore.

I wanted to protest and tell him no, that we could eat on our own time. We weren't on a date; it was an agreement, and I had waited long enough. But then I realized he just played a hard game and was probably starving.

"Okay," I smiled. "Something quick, please."

He winked at me, catching how needy I was. "Very quick."

Following him into the kitchen, I watched as he threw together a couple of sandwiches. He pointed me to the wine and I helped myself, pouring us each a glass.

Things were simple and easy. We laughed and talked about the game. I told him I was opening classes again and that I had an officer arranged for outside the door.

What had started off as a plan to ease our mutual sexual attraction for one another had turned into an actual date. Hours passed as we sat at his bar and talked. He told me a few things about growing up in a rough neighborhood and I told him the whole story of my mother and I being on our own.

"Now I just have to get her to come down for the show," I groaned as I mentioned how I locked down the theater for our recital.

"I can't believe you had to promise a celebrity," he snarled. "What do they get out of it?"

"Clout?" I mused. "I have no idea, but I waited too long to book something because I honestly wasn't sure I could keep the doors open. Until Mr. Peyton asked me to help you, I was losing money quicker than I was making it. Even with the classes and the students, the rent for that location is unbelievable. Then you add in paying the staff, the cleaning crew, the shoes, the music... it all adds up so quickly. And making up a fake grant and gifting to a few of the kids who need help paying for classes didn't help."

"Fuck, Miss Priss, you can't keep going like that," he pulled my hand into his and kissed my fingers.

"I know. I'm trying. I just took on a lot at once to make this place spark and it takes a lot to keep it going."

"You know, if you need..."

"No," I stopped him before he could say it. "Honestly, I'm making it sound worse than it is. I may have thought closing the doors to *Brise* may happen, but personally, I'm fine. It's just, no matter how much money one has, it isn't smart to keep losing money."

"So Coach found you and said he had a player that needed ballet lessons?"

"Pretty much," I smiled. "And you're doing pretty good since we started working together."

He shrugged his shoulders and looked a bit sheepish, "Maybe."

I was completely relaxed and happy, which was a different version of myself when I was with Ty. We had an entire conversation without me worrying about how I sounded or where my shoulders were. I didn't try overcorrecting my enunciations and I was positive I had never smiled as much as I had that night.

Ty stood up and took my hand, leading me to the middle of the living room. The lights were off, except for those over the bar where we had been sitting. Through the glass door, I could see a small balcony and in the distance was Atlanta's skyline. One of the best parts about living outside of the city was the remarkable view.

Ty fumbled with his phone for a minute while I gazed out the window. I had thought he was texting someone but when he tossed the phone to the couch, a slow song started playing over the speakers. He pulled me in close and held my hands and waist.

"Let me show you another way I can dance," he whispered as he started to sway.

"Isn't this a sad song?" I asked quietly, realizing he had turned on Anymore by Travis Tritt.

"I never thought of it that way. But it's one of my favorites."

His own interpretation of the song had me smiling to myself, a motion that he felt on his neck as we continued to dance. Our steps were juvenile in terms of dancing, but I had never felt like more of an adult.

We were dancing the best we could in the small space to a beautiful song in the room only lit up by the moonlight outside. Swallowing, I tamped down the romance and the intimacy we found ourselves in. I was under no illusions that we were becoming more, and I didn't want to accidentally fall for him as we held on to one another.

When the song ended, I felt Ty's lips gently caress the nape of my neck. Goosebumps formed on my skin and he nuzzled them with his nose. Another song started but it was not one I recognized, nor did it matter much.

Our dance was over.

Ty pulled away and led me down a short hallway with two closed doors. We entered the master bedroom and the first thing

I noticed was that it had a huge windows and the same view of the city. The only light we still had was the and it was all either of us needed.

Reaching behind him, Ty pulled his t-shirt over his head and tossed it onto the floor before reaching for his belt. As he popped the clasp from the holes, I lifted my own shirt over my head as well.

Ty's eyes widened when he saw my bright pink bra and my hard nipples trying to cut their way out of the fabric. Instead of finishing his belt, he left it loose and walked closer to me, running his thumb over my nipples.

I pushed into his touch, wanting more but not wanting to rush whatever was happening. It was different and as much as it scared me, I couldn't have backed away if I wanted to.

CHAPTER TWENTY-ONE

IT WAS the first time I had ever had someone in the stands to watch me play. It was also the first time I had someone waiting for me after the game. If that wasn't enough, I played well, scored a touchdown, and the media laid off my back in the post-game interview.

My plan was to get Giselle back to my place and fuck her senseless, but I was always starving after a game. I started to scarf down a quick sandwich, but as we sat there in my kitchen, we ended up talking and sharing. I learned so much more about Giselle Metrovik. She seemed so much more human and amiable.

Once I kissed her, though, she was a tiger and just as eager as I was to lose our clothes while we stumbled toward my bedroom. And as she stood in front of me in her pink lace I thought maybe I had died and gone to heaven.

Giselle was shaking with the need to touch me as her hands went up and fell back down. I imagined she was gathering the courage to take control, but was scared to be so bold.

My thumbs were still caressing her nipples as her tits sat in the palm of my hands. I didn't want to move, but decided to help her out and make her touch me. I lifted one of her hands to my chest, I placed it flat on my pec—over my heart. Swallowing hard, I soaked in the way her little hand tried squeezing the muscles on my chest.

The first time Giselle and I were together, we were ardent and impassioned. We moved on instinct and never questioned what was happening or what it meant. But we were almost acting as if we were kids, and unsure what to do next.

Unlike in her studio, I knew her better. We felt for connected and intimate. I wanted to make sure she was fucking happy and content.

Giselle had started rubbing her hand from my pec and around my body. She traced a few of my tattoos and watched her own fingers as they moved. I stayed in place, holding her, and gently teasing her nipple with my thumb.

We both looked up at one another at the same time and when our eyes locked, she blushed and bit her lip, embarrassment covering her features.

"Don't," I warned. "Don't stop."

There was not a trace of humor or insincerity in my voice. I wanted to do whatever the fuck she wanted, and I didn't want her questioning me, or herself.

Taking both her hands, I pressed them back onto my body and guided her around my shoulders, chest, and stomach. Then I hooked one of her hands into the waistband of my pants and left it there as I got closer to her.

When we were kissing, there were no hesitations, so I leaned down and pressed my lips to hers. With her fingers tucked into my waistband, she pulled me closer to her and wrapped her arms around my back the best she could. She took her nails and made goosebumps form over my body in every spot she touched.

Testing the theory of no panties, I undid the button of her jeans and tucked my hand in, running my fingers through the folds of her pussy. She was all skin and wetness inside her jeans and knowing she hadn't worn panties for me made me become rabid as I tried to get her jeans off her hips. We had to pull apart to get them off faster, and once they were thrown across my room, I lifted her off the floor and threw her onto my bed.

Hesitations were gone.

Her legs were spread wide and her arms were above her head. Although a few strands fell around her face, her hair was still tight in her bun. She looked down at my cock pushing on my jeans and licked her lips, causing me to almost come. I was no kid, and I had plenty of experience, but nothing would ever compare to the adolescent response I had to Giselle.

Falling to my knees at the end of the bed, I pulled her by the ankles until her legs wrapped around my neck and her wet pussy was directly in my face. Taking my tongue, I traced the seam of her folds and watched as she shook with need. She tasted so good, and when I pushed my tongue into her core, I was rewarded with her satisfied moans.

I could have spent a lifetime down there, making her happy. I wanted to draw out the feelings and keep my mouth on her forever. But as she shook with her impending orgasm, I pressed harder and let her come. Her hands found my hair and she pulled, screamed, and moved. Her pussy was grinding against my mouth and it took all I had not to rub my cock on the side of my bed.

When I knew she had all she could take, I rose up and wiped my mouth with the back of my forearm. My jeans were still on so I finished unbuttoning them and kicked them to the side. While she watched, I began stroking and showing her how hard I was for her.

She rose up on her knees and crawled to the end of the bed where I was standing. Then she braced herself on the edge with her hands.

"I want to taste you," she purred, then chastely kissed the tip. Her eyes shot up to mine and her tongue coated the underside of my cock. My knees were already weak with need. She was making it impossible to stand.

When her mouth opened around me, and her pink lips slid down my length, I growled like a damn lion. She used one hand to keep herself steady and the other at the base of my cock, stroking me where her mouth couldn't reach. I felt a tingle come up my spine and my thighs started shaking. If she didn't stop, I was going to come down her throat, and I wanted inside her pussy too much to let that happen.

With more force than I intended, I shoved her back, causing her to gasp and squeal as she landed on the bed. Climbing on top of her, I flipped her over and pulled her ass up into the air. If she was going to make me feel like an animal, we were going to fuck like animals.

My cock lined up with her core and I pushed hard, not giving her time to adjust before I pulled out and thrust back inside of her. The music was still on in the living room creating background noise to our grunts and moans, and the sound of our bodies slapping together. It was the perfect song for our perfect dance.

"Ty," Giselle moaned, almost a warning. "Ty…"

"Come with me, baby," I urged, knowing I was close to losing control.

While I kept a punishing pace, I took both hands and slapped down on her ass. It made her pussy clench tighter, and I knew I was done. "I'm about to fill this tight little pussy up, Miss Priss."

Before she started moaning again, I felt her pussy squeeze and I knew she was coming. Letting myself go, the relief and pleasure washed over me, causing me to get jerky and uncontrolled. If I was any less of the man I claimed to be, I would have shed a tear over how much I loved her pussy.

Touchdowns be damned.

Super Bowls could go fuck themselves.

I would give it all up to fuck Giselle for the rest of my life.

Feelings weren't something I was comfortable with and ruining that moment with feeling too much wasn't something I wanted to do, so I tamped my thoughts down and enjoyed it for what it was.

Whatever it was.

"I think I'm going to call Mrs. Watson and check on Reggie." Giselle was gently stroking her fingers across my chest as we laid in my bed.

"That's a good idea," I whispered, staring at the wall in front of me.

The reminder of Reggie made me think of Mike. Sam and I were more alike than I thought, since we both had older brothers caught in a web of poor decisions and dangerous situations.

For a while, every time my phone rang, I expected it to be the cops, or a hospital calling to tell me Mike was dead. When he escalated his business ventures, I knew one day he would run out of luck and run into someone more dangerous than he was.

Usually, when he came to Atlanta to visit, I loved it because it meant he was safe for a while. But with him there full time, it seemed he was out causing trouble, and it pissed me off.

When Giselle and I had been talking, I left out the part about Mike being as much trouble as he was. All she needed to know was that he and I had an unsettled relationship.

Admittedly, I had to give Mike credit. He left when he said he would. He kicked Marcus and Devon to the curb for crossing lines, even though I was sure they were way deeper lines than most people had. It still made me feel better that Mike had standards.

Smiling down at Giselle, I also thought about Mike being

interested in her. The odds of him seeing her and wanting to start something up with her were astronomical. Those odds were something that should have been running through my head more than they were. At that moment in time, all I could think of was how thankful I was that he backed off.

Every bit of me knew Giselle wouldn't give Mike the time of day, but fighting with my brother, and the risk of her pushing me away was much less with him out of that picture.

"Are you going to let me tell Sam you are a ballerina?" she giggled and it made me want to say *yes*. But that part of me was still on lockdown.

"No," I tickled her for good measure and she squealed. "That's our little secret, Miss Priss."

"Speaking of which, that touchdown dance was… something else."

"I thought it was damn impressive. I choreographed it just for you."

"As honored as I am, it gave me good insight into what we needed to work on in our next lesson." She leaned up on her elbow and looked down at me, smiling. "Lots and lots of *pas de chat* practice."

"Is that what I did? Shit, I'm better than I thought I was. I was just trying to jump."

Giselle leaned down and kissed me with soft pecks that started on my lips and led down to my chest. I let her do what she wanted, and took as much as I could before throwing the covers over our heads and rolling on top of her.

It wasn't planned to be so intimate, but I sunk myself deep inside of her and didn't want to move. We made love, slow and methodical. Sweet and tender. It was a first for me, and felt just as good as fucking her from behind had.

As Giselle fell asleep in my arms, I laid there and thought about how dangerous it would be to keep letting myself fall for her. I either needed to go for it, or back off completely. There was no easy answer. We were like night and day, the two of us would never work if we tried.

I was a street kid with a troubled past and a troubled family. The guy who didn't know how to love anyone because no one ever showed me what it was like. I didn't even know if I would recognize love if it slapped me in the face.

Giselle was first class, grade A, blue-ribbon, top tier. Opposites always attracted but outside of the bedroom, what good did that do?

The only thing I decided was that I couldn't just walk away. Not yet. I had a few more lessons with her and that should be enough time to know what was between us.

The following week, I had practice every day and dance lessons at my usual times. Giselle seemed more at ease with the security she had hired, and with the doors locked up tight at all times, no one could just pop in the way they had before.

On my lesson days, I snuck into the back of the reception area and watched Miss Priss do her thing with the kids. It amazed me how she could snap herself into ballerina mode, handle the kids, and make rockstar dancers out of them all in an hour.

Sam gave me high fives when he came from the studio each time. He seemed happier than I had seen him before, and I had to admit, he was good. Extremely good.

For an eleven-year-old, I was in awe of his poise and balance. He never had to be redirected, and each time Giselle started the music, it was as if he found a new level of astonishment. When I praised him afterward, he lit up even more and I realized I wielded a power I didn't know I had. He looked up to me more than he should have and if I had told him that I thought ballet sucked, he would have quit on the spot.

My attention to that detail didn't go unnoticed by Giselle. She walked perfectly composed into the lobby and bid everyone a good evening with her perfect words and poise. Then, as the last student left, she locked the door and turned to me with a smile. She thanked me for how I handled Sam and in an instant, she turned into the Giselle I met when our clothes were off.

She kissed me and shed her leotard, her hair came down, and we fucked in her office before we ever got to the dancing part of the evening.

After she redressed in leggings and a crop top, I would follow her out to the studio and once again, we would dance the way she wanted me to. I walked, leaped, twisted, turned, and darted the shit out of the moves she gave me.

My reward was smiles and kisses, which seemed like enough to make me the happiest man alive. But the additional praise she gave me was fun too. Her hand would cup my dick and squeeze, making me hard until I couldn't dance without fucking her again. Then I would tease her about touching her student inappropriately and she would tease me about everything in the world she could think of.

We laughed more than anything and we always ended the night with a slow dance. I walked her home but didn't go up. With practices and her schedule getting back to normal, we never made it an option. But that didn't mean we didn't want to.

Both of us would joke about canceling everything we had planned and laying in bed all day. If we didn't have others to answer to, we probably would have.

By the following Sunday, I had to leave town for an away game, but that didn't stop us from texting, talking, and FaceTiming. Giselle even watched my game on TV, and I did a touchdown dance especially for her.

Needless to say, we may have both thought we were going to

go our separate ways when I finished preseason and my dance lessons, but as time went on, I couldn't see that happening. We were a couple without saying the words or labeling ourselves.

As I started my last week of preseason and my lessons were ending, I had decided that there was never really anything to decide. There was no choice in the matter of letting her go because I couldn't if I tried. I needed her, and I needed to see what else there was between us.

But there was something that I had almost forgotten about completely. Something that could throw a wrench in my plans and my life. The one thing Giselle had no idea I dealt with.

My brother.

giselle

"THAT'S IT, JASMINE. PERFECT." I praised the tiny dancer as she nailed her *plié* while holding onto the barre along the mirror. Her form was excellent, and had improved immensely over a span of two weeks.

A lot had changed over the course of those two weeks.

For one, Ty and I were in sort of a relationship. We didn't exactly discuss the parameters in detail, but we spent almost every available moment either talking, texting, fucking, or dancing together. I wouldn't go as far as to say we were exclusive, but I would have been heartbroken if he told me he had plans with another woman.

Maybe it was not something either of us was looking for, but it found us, nonetheless. For Ty, as much as myself. He may not have said the words, but actions spoke louder than words.

No one had ever cared so much about my well-being and happiness. Ty tried every day to make me laugh—something he said I didn't do enough of when we first met. He brought me random things he knew I loved. He even made sure he was an amazing student when it was time to dance.

On the field, his game was back to the way it was before he

met me. At least, that was what the commentators said on TV. When Ty was asked what he had been doing to get back into form, he told them he was practicing a lot, and trying new ways to focus. That was true enough, and I accepted that as his answer.

I stopped needing validation for helping a star football player through the art of ballet. Initially, I wanted that nugget to add to the resume of my business, but I could understand why Ty didn't want all the guys he played with—and against—knowing he took ballet.

The main thing was, he was treating Sam like a rockstar for being a dancer, and Sam was eating it up. Sam had found his passion for dancing again and I knew Ty played a huge part in that.

Looking out of the window of the studio, I saw Ty exactly where I had seen him the last few times he had class. Leaning against the cubby wall, arms crossed, eyes on me. As all the mothers in the waiting area took sneak peeks at him and swooned when he smiled, my heart fluttered, knowing that the second all the kids left, I would be kissing him.

After our lesson, I wanted to finally ask him what we were. I needed to know what he was thinking, and if I had been imagining how much there was between us, or if he felt it as well.

Class ended and I walked into the lobby, curious what a few of the moms were talking to Ty about. One was asking about football, and the other touched his arm and asked what he was always doing hanging out in the dance studio.

He froze up for a minute because he didn't want to admit he had his own lessons, but his shoulders relaxed as he smiled up at me. "Just here to take my girl home."

I smiled, though I kept it stiff and hard because my prima ballerina ego was still in check. But inside, I was melting, warm, and I lifted my chin a little higher. As unnecessary as it was, my brain was screaming, *"That's right, back up bitch."*

Ty did to me.

Everyone made their way out, and just like every other time, Ty locked the door securely behind them. I had walked into my office to change, but he found me and stopped me.

"Leave that on tonight. The Miss Priss look makes me fucking hard."

I rolled my eyes, feeling myself slowly morph into the Giselle I was when he was around. I stopped undressing and met him in the middle of the room, wrapping my arms around his waist and looked up at him. "Everything makes you hard."

"You're not wrong," he winked and pecked my lips.

"You sure you have to leave Saturday?" I sounded needy but Ty didn't seem to mind.

"Yeah, baby," he ran a hand down my face and patted my lip with his fingertip. "One more away game of preseason, and then home for two weeks to kick off the year."

"Come home with me tonight, then?"

"Fuck yeah," he whispered as he leaned down to kiss me gently.

This was normally the part where our kiss grew and I ended up naked underneath Ty on my couch or desk. With him coming to my place later, we got started on the lesson so we could hurry home.

"This is your last class," I turned my mouth down in a frown as we walked onto the dance floor.

"I learned a lot," Ty did a leap and twirled around. It was not bad for a big guy like Ty with limited practice. He had learned a few basics, and that was all we had really set out to do. We fixed a few of his problems with his flat feet, and as long as he remembered to channel his focus on his leaps as much as he did the ball and the other team, he would have an amazing season.

"What am I going to do next week when no one is here to walk me home," I joked but I was serious at the same time. I didn't want to have our conversation right then, I wanted to wait till we were at my place, but ending our lessons was a heartbreak in and of itself.

"Oh baby," Ty grabbed my shoulders and looked down into my eyes. "I still plan on being here every Tuesday and Thursday whether you want me to be or not. We don't have to do ballet, but we can find other ways to dance." His eyebrows shot up and down, and the smirk he gave me was playful and full of promise.

"Really?" I teased. "Can we do the lift from Dirty Dancing?"

Ty pulled back slightly and looked as if he was thinking for a minute. "Oh, fuck yeah. We don't have to wait, though." He took my waist in his hands and lifted me over his head effortlessly while I screamed and laughed.

I must have been louder than I intended because as Ty set me down on my feet again, the guard outside started banging on the locked door.

"Shit," Ty turned. "We better both go so he knows I didn't murder you."

We walked quickly to the door as the guard continued to bang, "Miss Metrovik? Miss Metrovik? Are you ok?"

I opened the door, barely missing his fist as it flew to bang the door one more time. "I'm ok, I'm ok."

He was looking behind me where Ty had approached and was looking out of the door over to top of my head.

"Sorry," Ty said easily before trailing off. "I..."

He never finished his thought. His eyes were focused on something I couldn't see at my level and I tried looking around the guard. Ty never said anything else or indicated what the problem was, though.

"Ty?" I asked, hoping to snap him out of it, wanting him to explain what was happening.

"It's okay," he said, pulling me back inside. He started to close the door but then looked to the guard. "Go ahead and take off, man. I got it from here."

The guard nodded and looked to me for approval. I was too

confused to worry about why Ty was telling him to leave, so I nodded and let Ty close the door.

Pacing across the lobby, he looked like a caged animal with serious decisions to make. I let him go back and forth a few times but eventually, I needed to know what the hell was going on.

"Ty?" He stopped and looked at me, tilting his head but still lost in thought. "What's going on?"

"I think I saw someone," he looked toward the closed door and then back to me.

"Then why would you send the guard away?" I had taken my voice up a pitch with the nerves flowing through me.

"Not anyone dangerous," he said calmly. "I sent him away because I think we should skip dancing tonight."

"But why?" I didn't understand. If someone was creeping around that wasn't dangerous, why leave? Nothing made sense.

"You know what?" Ty started putting his shoes back on and nodding at my office. "Go grab your things and I'll be back in five minutes. I won't take my eyes off that door, but I just want to see if it was my brother I saw walking by across the street."

"Your brother?" I calmed down. Ty had told me he and his brother had a strange relationship. He worried about him and mentioned that he hadn't heard from him since he moved out of his apartment.

My first thought was, they were having issues and when he saw his brother, he decided it was fate and he needed to talk to him. My second thought was, maybe his brother found *him* and was hoping Ty would give him time to talk.

As connected as I felt to Ty, we were not near close enough for me to insist he not talk to him at that moment. I had a bad feeling but I needed to trust Ty. His brother was his problem, not mine.

"Ok," I agreed.

He kissed my cheek, told me he would be right back and darted out of the door, leaving me standing there in confusion.

After grabbing my things from the office, I made my way back into the lobby. Ty was still not back so I took the time to log off the computer and turn the lights off in the studio.

Just as I emerged from the studio, the door opened and I turned with a smile, ready to praise Ty's timing and hear how things went.

But it wasn't Ty that came barreling through the door. It was another man holding a gun and a snarl on his face. It was a different man than before and he shut the door quickly, locking us in.

Before I could scream, his hand was over my mouth in an instant and the gun was pointed at my temple as he backed me into the room.

"Where is it?" he demanded.

I shook my head, having no clue what he meant. Where was what? I couldn't ask because his hand covered my mouth but the moaning I emitted told him I didn't know.

"Where is it, bitch?" He tugged on my face, straining my neck and pressing the gun harder into the side of my head.

"I don't know what you are talking about," I cried, although it was muffled and barely understandable.

"The stash. Where is it?"

I screamed the best I could, hoping Ty could hear me through the door.

"Oh sweetheart," the guy said into my ear. "You are extremely dumb."

He was laughing as I shrugged against his hold. He started walking me closer to the door where the blinds were closed. He took the gun from my head long enough to create a peephole in the blinds and forced me to look outside.

I saw Ty, with his back almost turned all the way to the studio. He was laughing and bro-hugging a man who looked almost exactly like him and eerily familiar.

Their conversation seemed happy and excited. Ty was

laughing at everything he said and since I was concentrating so much on Ty, I almost missed it.

The other guy, Ty's brother. He was the one who came into *Brise* that first time. He was the one that hit me and made me blackout.

"See, Princess. Ty isn't going to come save you. He's part of the plan."

I was shaking my head no, refusing to believe him, but it was hard since Ty wasn't coming back. He wasn't watching the door like he said he would and he sent the guard home.

It was his last night in the studio and his last chance to see to it that whatever they wanted from me, they got. That was all I could think about, and the blood drained from my face at how much sense it made.

"Now where is my package?"

"I honestly don't know what you are talking about," I pleaded.

"Bitch," the guy said one more time. "If I haven't found it by the time you wake up, you're taking a bullet between the eyes. You messed with the wrong motherfuckers."

Wake up? I was confused, but just for a second. Things became clear when he raised the butt of the gun and hit me with it, causing me to once again blackout.

Causing me to be silent.

CHAPTER TWENTY-THREE

"YO!" I yelled, using a language my brother understood.

He walked up to the edge of the sidewalk to meet me, emerging from the darkness of the park. "Hey bro."

"Hey bro? What the hell are you doing here, Mike?"

He looked confused and a little hurt at what I guessed was the wrong question.

"Calm down man, I was waiting on you, hoping we could talk."

"Why? I've been trying to call you for over a week. Why not answer your phone if you need to talk to me? How did you know I was here?"

Mike smiled and shook his head, clearly finding me amusing. "Dude, the way you looked talking about the ballerina? Yeah, I knew exactly where to find you."

I started to shout things like, *"How did you know when I would be here?"* And *"Why do I always find you on this side of town?"* But it didn't really matter, Mike always had a flair for the dramatics. If he wanted to talk to me, especially about Giselle, then he was exactly where he wanted to be.

"So, what is it you wanna talk about?"

He smiled again, looking almost proud. "I knew you liked her. Just wanted to see for myself."

"You couldn't knock or call like a normal human?"

"Calm down, man, what's up your ass?" He slid his hands casually into his pockets and looked back at *Brise*. My eyes followed his, noticing the door was still closed and all was quiet over there.

"Look, Giselle has had some people breaking into her place. We are all on high alert on this side of town."

His eyes got wide in disbelief and he looked back and forth a million times. "No shit?"

"Yeah, so, when I saw someone out here, I thought it may be whoever was busting in on her."

"Man, I'm so fucking sorry, little bro. Shit, I was just trying to catch you when you left, I swear." My brother was a liar, but not usually to me. He chose to not say anything if he thought he needed to lie. So, like an idiot, I instantly believed him. I still wanted nothing more than to see the good in my brother. With Marc and Dev gone, I wondered who he was hanging with, or if he was alone.

"Why haven't you answered my calls?"

He reached in his pocket and lifted his phone into his hand. The glass was dark and I could barely read what the screen said, so he turned us a little so the light from the sidewalk shined down onto the phone.

"Inactive?" I questioned. "What happened?'

"Times are a little tough, bro. I want to make a life here in Atlanta and I know you don't always agree with my business, but making Marc and Dev leave meant business slowed." I eyed him, lost in his story as he kept quietly explaining. "Phone went out sometime last week and I've been too proud to stop by. I guess tonight, I just got too curious and wanted to catch you while I could."

For some reason, I laughed—hard. Mike shook his head and

started laughing too. For all the bullshit we faced in our lives, my heart was breaking thinking of Mike not having a fucking phone.

Shit, the irony.

I pulled him into a quick hug and stepped back to look at him. "Fuck that. You need me to get the phone turned back on? You fucking come ask. You need anything, you ask. We don't live on those streets anymore. We don't have to live together for me to care about you."

Mike was laughing and play-punching me, trying to shake off his somber story. "I know, but I'll get it back on. I'll get things going."

"Well to answer your question, yeah, I'm crazy about Miss Ballerina in there." I started to look back at *Brise*, but Mike pulled me into another hug.

"Fuck yeah. Not gonna lie, I was hoping you broke her heart so I could pick up the pieces."

I pulled from him and punched his shoulder, laughing some more and feeling good about the chat we were having. It took a weight off my shoulders knowing he was okay and that the only problem he had—his phone—was one I could fix easily.

"I really like her. A lot. I know she is way out of my league and sometimes, I worry she really does have a stick up her ass. But even that side of her is something I crave."

"I'm fucking happy for you. Honestly. I'm sad for me," he joked and winked at me. "But happy for you."

As much as I loved catching up with Mike, I promised Giselle I wouldn't take too long and it was already longer than I wanted. An idea popped in my mind, though.

"I gotta go get Giselle and walk her home. How about you hang here for a minute while I get her? You can meet her and walk with us."

"Shit. Meeting the family? Must be serious." Mike put his hand behind his neck and started rubbing, unsure about what he wanted to say. "You think it's a good idea letting her meet the low-life brother?"

"Come on man. It doesn't have to be like that," I shook my head and smirked at him, daring him to argue with me.

"Yeah, it does," he got serious and straightened his shoulders. "Because that bitch has a hundred thousand dollars' worth of my drugs, and if I don't get them back, the princess won't be doing much twirling."

"Whoa!" I held my hand up to stop him, praying he was joking. In fact, I knew he was joking. Because there was no way my brother was that demented. No way he was that cruel.

Drugs? Yeah I saw that.

But hurting Giselle? No way.

Threatening someone I was in love with? He wouldn't.

But if he wasn't joking, and he was dead serious, then that would mean our entire conversation was a…setup.

With that, I started to back away and run toward the door to *Brise*. I needed to get to her and take her home. Keep her safe. I also needed to make peace with the fact that I may end up calling the cops on Mike. If he was serious about his threats, then I could no longer turn a blind eye. I loved him and I let him get away with too much shit. But with Giselle in my life, I had something to be better for, something to keep me on the right side of the tracks.

As I took off toward the door, I reached for my phone in my pocket but realized it wasn't with me. It was inside, sitting on the counter where I forgot to get it when I walked out to confront my brother.

I pulled on the door, urging it open but she must have secured the lock after I left. So I banged and called for her, "Open up baby, it's me."

There was nothing but silence.

"Giselle, open the door. Let's go home."

"You know what the best part is?" My brother yelled from

across the street. I looked back and he was watching me with a smile on his face, laughter in his features. His hands were still tucked in his pockets and he looked like he was watching ducks scurry across the road with how calm he was.

I turned to face him, letting him laugh at me and tell me I was nuts. That he was joking. He would never forgive me for believing him so easily, but fuck him for even pretending he would hurt her.

"The best part is," he continued, "was that you saw me and sent that fucking cop away. You made it so fucking easy. Honestly, I couldn't have even planned something this smooth."

"What the fuck, Mike? What do you want?"

"I told you. She has my stash," he seethed. "But since you love her and all, I promise I won't hurt her if she gives it to me peacefully."

"Bro, she doesn't have any drugs."

"Bro," he mocked me. "I put them in there myself a few weeks ago. Right after I knocked her out cold. When I went back, the bitch was hiding and the only reason I didn't press was because I realized you were the fool in there with her. I gave you time to get out of her pussy and away from the line of fire. I gave you that chance."

"That was you?" It made sense. Why Giselle screamed when she first saw me. Mike and I looked a lot alike in skin tone and height. Some of our features were similar. We definitely looked related.

Then when I heard his voice as I hid with Giselle behind the counter, I knew it was familiar. Although it sounded muffled and I couldn't place it at the time.

It would also explain his true intentions of trying to enter *Brise* that morning I saw him, and why he eyed me so vehemently.

"Wait, are you the one that took the drugs?" He asked me, like a bulb just went off in his head as well. "You know how to run drugs just as well as I do. Did you take them in case you tanked your football career?"

"You motherfucker," I wasn't going to run toward him, I wasn't leaving that door. I looked around for someone, anyone, that was passing through so I could yell at them to call the cops.

But it was too late at night, and it was actually supposed to be a quiet part of town. Most people were home and in bed, getting ready to work the next day. No one was just walking around unless they had shady business to attend to.

"One more thing," Mike yelled as he raised a very working phone to his ear. He mumbled in it and then stashed it back into his pocket before finishing his thought to me. "Times up."

At his words, I heard a gunshot behind me. Giselle was in there and she wasn't alone. It took me an instant to hate myself for turning my back on that door. A combination of fear and self-loathing seemed to be snaking its way through my chest.

"Giselle!" I screamed again, so loud I hoped I could be heard on the other side of the mile-long park.

I started pounding at the glass on the door, urging it to break. If it shattered, my football season would shatter with it because I would be sliced into a million pieces. Still, I beat on it and begged. I sure as fuck didn't want to leave her alone with my brother lurking and someone else inside, but I had no choice, I was going to have to run for help.

Looking back at where my brother was standing, I noticed he was gone.

Disappeared.

There was nothing but stark darkness and still air.

Someone was still inside with Giselle, but I could no longer worry about who or whether they would get away. I had to run, I had to find help. There was a flashing *open* sign the next block over and I started a full sprint, hoping they were actually open and would call the police.

By the time I approached, I realized it was a mom and pop sandwich shop that closed at nine and had just left their light on.

Fuck!

I kept running, knowing if I got to the other side of the park, there were always people milling around out there. It was Atlanta, one of the biggest cities in the United States. Giselle's corner was quiet, but that didn't mean the city was abandoned. I just had to get across the park.

When I was sprinting down the road and attempting to cut across the middle of the park, police cars started coming by, racing to get to the direction I had just come from. Considering someone must have heard the shot and called the police, I ran back, hoping to see that Giselle was safe, that the shot had been a warning. Because I was still in denial that my brother would kill or hurt her.

As I approached, the cops had already surrounded the area and one of them stopped me from going any farther.

"Sir, this is an active crime scene. You will have to turn around."

"My girlfriend is in there. There were shots fired and I went to get someone."

"Your girlfriend was the one shot?"

"She was hit?"

"Sir, I will have a detective come talk to you. We can't let you past because this is an active crime scene and we need to keep it secure." He turned to head back toward *Brise* but must have taken pity on me because he stopped and added, "And yes, someone was hurt. I'm not sure of the extent, but the woman will be transported to the hospital as soon as possible."

CHAPTER TWENTY-FOUR

THIS WAS what I got for always turning my head where my brother was concerned. The day I decided to *not* be a part of his shady side of life, I should have turned away from him completely. Trying to keep a relationship with him was hard, but I continued to do so because he was all I had.

Even as the detective came to question me, I waffled on whether or not to out Mike's role in the evening, or if I could let the gunman be hung by himself. It was just that brotherly instinct that had kicked in the second they asked me what I knew.

My gut said that Mike was depending on that side of me shining. As evil as his words were to me, we had connected and shared a moment before it all went to shit. Even if it was fake to him, it was real to me.

If his intent was to scare me, then he succeeded.

But he had no idea how deep it ran for me and Giselle. Hell, I hadn't even realized it until that moment. When I looked across that street at him, holding up a second phone that clearly worked. He had no idea that I would have shot him myself if it meant saving her.

So I told the detective the truth.

Luckily, he was the same detective Giselle and I called the night Mike made his way into *Brise* for the second time. He knew she and I were close and knew I had been with her when the second break-in happened. I even told him about Mike trying to enter *Brise* the day Giselle had been late, and that he told me he was there because he was crushing on Giselle. I suspected he was trying to collect whatever he left there the first time, though.

Still, the detective seemed stoic and angry.

At me.

Fuck, I guess I couldn't blame him, I was angry at me too.

For a moment, I had been so worried about my brother that I let my guard down where Giselle was concerned. I sent her hired guard away, I left her alone, and in the end, she was hurt because I sat out there laughing with my brother for too long.

"I need to know if she's okay," I pleaded, tired of talking about it and wanting to know more about how she was.

"She was shot," the detective snapped. "How the hell do you think she's doing?"

The blood drained from my face because until he said that, I had hoped the gunshot was a scare tactic. I had hoped the other officer was wrong. I had hoped that the other person in there was a woman and Giselle had overpowered her. I had hoped for anything other than what was so glaringly obvious and so over-whelmingly painful.

"Is she alive?" I yelled. If he told me, "*No,*" then Mike and whoever he had working with him was dead.

I would kill them myself.

Maybe they thought I wasn't capable of their level of sin because I didn't involve myself after going off to college. Maybe they thought I was soft. True, I had hidden behind football and the expectations that Coach had for me to stay on the right side of the tracks. Football motivated me.

In the blink of an eye, that was no longer my motivation.

It was Giselle.

And if she lost her life at the hands of someone I was capable of confronting, then that poor bastard had no idea what was coming.

"She's alive and responsive," he assured me.

"I'm headed to the hospital," I shoved passed him on the sidewalk, not far from where I had been talking to Mike before everything happened. There were too many emergency vehicles to see *Brise* but I knew an ambulance had left with her before the detective had shown up to talk to me.

"Just one problem with that," the detective called, making me stop and turn back to look at him. "She asked us to keep you away. So we cannot allow you near her."

"What?" I yelled, louder than I had been before. I stomped back toward the detective and he placed a hand on his holstered gun, stopping me from wrapping my hands around his neck. "I was there, she needs me."

"We have called an emergency contact to be with her. But she adamantly said to keep you away."

"Did she say why?" I was so fucking mad, but so fucking relieved she was coherent enough to even speak at all.

"No, she didn't. But she seemed scared."

"She knows it's Mike," I mumbled. "She knows it's my brother and she's fucking scared."

I didn't have my keys or my phone, not even my wallet. All of those were still being secured by the police inside *Brise*. I could walk to the fucking hospital, but I didn't want to risk scaring Giselle by showing up.

So I stomped across the park and headed into her building. I got on the elevator and hit the button for the top floor.

The elevator lifted up quickly since it was late and no one else was trying to hit the buttons, so before I knew it, the doors were opening to the apartments on the top floor.

Marching straight to the second door, I started banging and

yelling, loud enough I wouldn't be surprised if the neighbors heard me in the other apartment.

After a few minutes, the door flew open and Coach was standing there in nothing but his boxers, rubbing the sleep from his face.

"What the fuck?" He yelled, before calming a bit when he saw the state I was in.

"Giselle was shot," I breathed.

His eyes widened and he moved so I could enter the apartment. I had only ever been there once and it was when I needed to drop something off to Coach.

As close as Coach and I had gotten, it wasn't normal for a player to hang out with their coach. It was like a boss hanging with the people they supervised. In most workplaces, it created a blurry line and we were no different.

But when it came down to it, Coach treated us like a dad, or an older brother would, and that was why he pulled me in and sat me down. He poured me some water and sat with me as I started to explain the whole evening.

From the first night Giselle and Coach met, right down to the morning I was hiding in Giselle's apartment when he knocked, I left no stone unturned. It wasn't a matter of saving my football career by distancing myself from Mike, or what would inevitably be a media storm.

It was about Coach being the only other person in town that knew both me and Giselle. He was the only person I trusted and the only person I could turn to. I needed him to help me figure out what was going on. I needed him to talk to her, check on her, and make sure she got whatever she wanted.

I assumed they had called her mom, but I was still unclear on how well they got along. Maybe that didn't matter in these circumstances. Maybe she would drop everything and come to be with her.

But I knew in my case, if I had been buried six feet deep, neither my mom nor dad would give two shits.

"Fuck!" Coach started pacing. The loose sweatpants he had put on made him look less like my coach and more like a regular friend. "This is all my fault."

I wasn't expecting that to come out of his mouth and I wasn't sure why in the hell he thought he was at fault. Because he involved me? Fuck, that couldn't be true because my presence alone had saved Giselle on more than one occasion.

My being there was a fucking gift.

Until I let her down.

"The night I met her, I knew something was off. She was frazzled and a little disheveled. Shit I originally stopped her to ask if she was okay. But the moment she spoke, she seemed fine. Completely. She carried herself perfectly and was so poised and put together that any concerns I had immediately fell away."

"That's her 'Ballerina Facade,'" I bit, almost angry with her for being so good at being perfect. "She would never have let you see her undone."

"I just assumed she was tired. She was still dressed as if she had just got off work and the more I spoke to her, the more I let any worry about her fall away. I ended up being more worried about what she could do for you."

"It didn't matter, there wasn't anything we could have done that first night. She had already called the cops and we had no way of knowing Mike was behind it."

With everything we knew, I just didn't understand how he thought any of it was his fault. All he did was ask her to give me ballet lessons.

Then again, Coach was Coach. He may not have been *her* coach but he was a good guy that took care of everyone around him. Almost to a fault.

He never looked after himself and I assumed that was how he

was so successful as a younger coach in the league, but lacked many significant people in his personal life.

"So wait," he leaned back and eyed me. "You were there the morning I stopped by?"

I snorted, the first semi-laugh I attempted since the night went to shit. "I was hiding behind her couch like you had X-ray vision and when I pulled her down, she just hid with me."

That was the first time I realized I could fall for her.

"Because you knew I would ring your neck for fucking your dance instructor?"

"I know how protective you get of people in your circle. I knew if you were asking her to do you a favor, then you wouldn't want me fucking it up by being a dick."

"Were you a dick? Seriously think about it Ty. You have a bad rap sheet when it comes to being 'nice.' Maybe that's why she doesn't want to see you."

I was shaking my head no before he even finished his thought. That wasn't it. Maybe I was thinking we were more than she thought we were. I could accept that since we hadn't talked about *us*, that maybe she was pushing me away to save herself. Maybe she thought she was doing me a favor so I didn't feel obligated.

But it wasn't because I was a dick to her.

"I don't think you get it Coach. I'm in love with that woman."

Coach was taking a sip of his drink and almost spewed it everywhere. "What?"

My glass was empty so I circled my finger around the top of the glass, mindlessly. I was looking down, not wanting to look him in the eye when I said those words.

In all my macho glory, I was still a fucking coward. I could admit that I fell for Giselle, but I didn't have it in me to make it a big deal, to be overly dramatic about it.

I never answered Coach. He wasn't really wanting me to repeat my words, anyway. He was just as stunned as everyone else, including myself, that I had finally found a woman I would trade football for.

"Can you check on her, please?"

"I can try. Fuck, I'll do my best." He stood up and pointed to the couch, "Sleep there. I'll go up there in the morning. There isn't shit I can do tonight."

I looked at the clock and it was already 2 am. Time had been lost while everything was happening and I couldn't believe that much time had passed. I wasn't even sure what time I had gotten to Coach's house.

Sleep wasn't happening though. Every emotion from guilt to sadness to anger to rage was coursing through me. I stared at Coach's ceiling all night and talked myself out of storming the hospital at least 700 times. A part of me felt that laying there was not the best idea, that I should be manic and fighting to see her.

The bigger part of me just didn't want to scare her or risk not being able to see her at all when the time came. I wanted to save my irrational decisions for when I saw Mike again. He was the one that would get the worst of me.

At six am, I had decided four hours of misery and idleness had been enough. I got up and walked straight into Coach's room, not bothering knocking. The plan was to wake him up and have him help me get to Giselle. I needed to see her more than I needed anything. But to my surprise, he was already dressed, standing in his room as he threw a shirt on.

"Fuck, Ty. Knock next time?"

"Ready?" I didn't bother acknowledging his statement or asking why he was awake. If he was ready to go, then I was too.

"You can ride with me to the hospital, Ty. I will do everything I can to figure out what the update is. But please don't make me regret taking you."

"Cross my heart," I lied.

giselle

GETTING shot in the leg was a dancer's worst nightmare.

Being dead would have been a better outcome. Especially since my heart would be dead with the rest of me.

My very broken heart.

It was Ty's brother who was helping himself to the cover of my studio. It was him that was hurting me, threatening me, scaring me, and causing my entire life to be chaos. If that wasn't enough, I had to consider that Ty may have been helping him.

Honestly, I wasn't sure how much he was involved in his brother's tryst, but I knew he was helping him in some capacity. He didn't just didn't anticipate feeling the way he did for me.

Just like I didn't plan on falling for him.

Tyson Black, the bad boy of the NFL. They guy with trouble tattooed all over him. The guy that when it came down to it, chose trouble over what we were developing between us.

I had been out of surgery for a few hours. It wasn't dire or life threatening, so they removed the bullet and stitched me up in no time. According to the doctor, I would need to rest and rehab but I should be back to normal in no time.

But it was still too long. The set back meant, once again, I was failing *Brise* and failing the kids. My heart twisted again for the kids not getting to do their show, but I found a little relief in having a good excuse to let *Brise* go once and for all.

Trying to replace the stage with teaching hadn't been as seamless as I thought it would be. Maybe it was because my heart was no longer into being Miss Perfect all the time. If being with Ty showed me anything, it was that I started *Brise* because it was what I thought would be best for my skill set, but I hated the front I always carried.

Ty broke through those walls and I was still okay—still me. In fact, I was able to be me and continue to teach the kids at a professional level. I even found out that I really liked teaching football players how to dance. Sex with Ty was one thing, but the high I got from watching him utilizing what he thought of as "feminine" dance steps was something I hadn't expected.

I knew athletes of all sports used the lessons in ballet to help in their own sports, but Ty was my first attempt at seeing it first-hand, and it was amazing. I had even talked to Mr. Peyton about helping one of their other tight ends in the future.

Of course, with everything that had happened, there was no way I could take him up on helping another one of his players. I would inevitably be around Ty and that could never happen.

Not that it mattered since I was most likely going to have to close *Brise* and head back to New York for a while.

In the meantime, I laid in that hospital bed and contemplated where I went from there. It had been less than 12 hours since Ty walked out that door to "inspect" things and my world had been flipped upside down. It was too fresh to be making life decisions, but I had nothing else to do while laying there.

"Miss Metrovik?" I looked up as I heard the nurse enter the room. "You have a man here to see you, but he's not a family member so we cannot let him up unless you ask to see him."

Ty, it was Ty and I didn't want to see him at all. I had already come to terms with the fact that when it came time to speak with the police again, I wouldn't tell them the role I was told he played. I wouldn't tell them anything about Ty.

I had no proof he knew what was going on, and I wanted to keep pretending he had no clue. Was I an idiot for that? Sure I was. But that is what love did to you, it made you stupid.

No matter how involved Ty was, falling for him was not fake, and that part of me was stupid enough to protect him.

However, I couldn't face him. Not now and maybe not ever. I would believe anything he told me. Footballs are round, the sun is cold, dogs go moo. I would believe it all, and until I was sure where I stood, I needed to protect myself.

So no, Ty couldn't be there.

"His name is Levi Peyton," the nurse continued, snapping me out of my thoughts.

"Mr. Peyton?" Shit, did I want to see him?

"Yes ma'am," she smiled. "Goooood looking man. Fine. Sexy. Mmmm Hmmm."

I smiled at her enthusiasm in what I was sure was an actual attempt to make me smile. The lighter moment gave me a chance to stop panicking and decide on instinct. "I want to see Mr. Peyton."

"I bet you do," she winked. "I'll go get him."

While she was gone, the panic set back in. What was I going to tell him? How much did he know?

I guess it didn't matter. He knew enough that he was at the hospital first thing in the morning and I could only assume it was Ty that told him where I was.

Seeing him would allow me to see Ty, in a way. I could get an update and then explain why I couldn't see Ty. The one thing I was sure of was that Ty respected Mr. Peyton. If I could appeal to him to tell Ty to let me be, then Ty would.

"Knock knock," I heard his voice as he entered and I smiled up at him. "Damn, you look amazing for a woman that just got shot."

I was instantly thankful that he was not uptight and sorrowful. I didn't want to mourn last night, I wanted to move forward.

"Hi Mr. Peyton. Please come in." I wasn't sure which version of me Mr. Peyton was going to get. I owed him my professionalism, but I was laid in a hospital bed and I was almost one thousand percent sure he knew I slept with his number one tight end.

"Shit, Giselle," he was coming toward me, looking at me with friendly eyes.

"Right?" I tried to laugh and wave at my leg but it was covered with a blanket.

"Tell me everything."

"Can I ask how you knew I was here, first?"

He smiled and sat down in the chair next to the bed. "You know the answer to that."

"Yeah," I nodded, "I do."

"He's worried sick, ya know? He came banging on my door last night and told me what happened. He was a mess, but we knew from the detective that you were alive. He still didn't sleep a wink and I didn't either, if I'm being honest."

"I don't remember much," I confessed. "The guy entered the studio and Ty was outside talking to his brother. I don't remember much after that. I just remember waking up on the gurney with a pain in my head and leg."

He took his hands and wiped over his face a few times before looking back up at me. He didn't speak but I could tell he didn't really know what to say to all that.

"I don't want to see Ty," I confessed. "I don't trust myself around him, and I need time to sort this all out."

He was nodding and biting his lip, looking around the room remaining silent.

"I don't know if he was a part of all this, but the guy that entered the room told me he was."

"He wasn't," Mr. Peyton said quickly. "His brother is a piece of shit, but Ty is the younger brother that despite his fortune and fame, still wants his big brother to be his brother.”

“Then how do we really know?”

“You tell me. Do you really think he would do this to you? Be a part of anything that would hurt you?”

“He told you everything, didn’t he?”

Mr. Peyton’s bottom lip frowned a bit in sadness as he nodded, “Yeah he did. And trust me, he didn't want anything to happen to you. He didn't know what was going on. Everything that happened after Ty heard that gunshot has sent him into such a tailspin that I’m not sure even football can heal him.”

The details of what actually happened had not yet been explained to me properly. So I scrunched my nose in confusion.

“Ty said he sent the guard away because he saw his brother and decided you two should leave. He felt Mike was harmless enough, and was going to ask him what was up before you two left. He lured Ty in with some brotherly love, and then told him you had his drugs. Once Ty realized it was a setup, he ran back but the door was locked and he heard the gunshot. Apparently, he ran around trying to find someone to call 911. The guy that lives above your studio heard the gunshot and called, though.”

Tears were streaming down as Mr. Peyton relayed what Ty had told him. Ty’s version was sad, and painful. If that was how it went for Ty, my heart broke for him as I pictured him running to get help.

“He told the detectives everything. All about Mike and his dealings, everything Mike and he spoke about last night. I haven't heard anything today, but I am willing to bet Mike has a warrant and an APB out on him.”

More tears fell along with relief.

“He really wants to see you, Giselle. But I told him if I got to talk to you, that I would do whatever you asked of me. I will relay whatever you let me.”

I shook my head as more tears fell. “I can’t see him, Mr.

Peyton. I love him too much to trust myself around him. I want to heal first. Mentally and Physically."

Mr. Peyton nodded one time and stood up. "You got it."

"But please don't tell him that one part," I added quickly, hoping he understood I meant the part about loving him. I didn't want to explain why, but luckily, he didn't ask. He smiled and leaned down to kiss my cheek before telling me he would be back at another time to check in.

I understood why Ty looked up to him. He was hard-nosed and tough, but strong and honorable. I was willing to bet Mr. Peyton never did anything wrong or broke any rules. He was just that type of guy.

It was not a minute after Mr. Peyton left that the door opened again and my mother ran to me. In fact, it was so quick, they probably had passed one another in the hall.

"Oh my sweet darling!"

I told the police to call her, I begged them. I knew she would hop on the first flight to come see me. Maybe our relationship was an odd one, but no one wanted to be without their mom.

"Mom," I cried, wanting her to comfort me the way only moms could. She leaned down and hugged me gently before placing a kiss on my head.

I hadn't seen her in so long. Moving to Atlanta had made it hard and until I saw her face without a screen between us, I didn't realize how much I had missed her.

"God, please tell me everything," she insisted, pulling away and dabbing her eyes. I wasn't even sure if her tears were real. Galena Metrovik had a flair for theatrics.

However, I knew her concern was real.

"Oh Mom. It's a long story. You better sit down."

She sat and crossed her legs, making sure her perfect pantsuit wasn't creased as I began talking. I started from the beginning and told her everything, including agreeing to help a football player in order to pad the account at *Brise*.

I told her about the break ins, hiring a guard, being unsure if *Brise* was the right move for me, being worried about the kids, even the part about falling for Ty. I left nothing out, and I expected her to chastise me and tell me she told me so, that I belonged on the stage.

After telling her about Ty, I even expected her to be disappointed in me. In my entire life, my mom had never been in love. At least not that I knew of. She had men coming in and out of her life, but love wasn't something she ever admitted to. Her only true love was dancing, and I guess me.

So I finished and sat back, waiting to hear her dismay in my choices. I watched her eyes get wide, her hand covering her lips. I think I even saw a real tear as she shook her head at my story. She swallowed and looked around the room, looking out of sorts. She was clearly at a loss for words, and it was only a matter of time before she found them.

"Sorry if I have disappointed you, Mom. *Brise* was a…"

"No," she finally spoke up, cutting me off with a stern tone. "You will not apologize to me for, well, anything. I am incredibly proud of you, almost envious."

My jaw dropped and it was my turn to be at a loss for words.

"Darling, you are one of the world's best dancers. But that is probably because of genetics and the fact that you were raised by someone who was always dancing. That doesn't mean it is what you were meant to do."

"Mom, I love dancing. I love teaching. I want *Brise* to be successful, I really do. But there is just no way I can keep it up at this rate. Things were looking better, then the break-ins, and now this," I pointed to my leg. "I cannot teach like this. The kids will lose their recital, I will owe the theater too much money, I will—"

"Stop, right now." She cut me off. "We will figure all of that out. You just rest and get better. There is not anything you can do until then."

I swallowed hard and nodded, so thankful she was with me.

"You came quick," I changed the subject.

"Darling, an officer called to tell me my child had been shot. Yes, I came very quick." She spoke like I was an idiot, like it was a no-brainer. But again, with her, I never knew.

Or maybe I just always assumed. Without the stress of the stage, we were both different people. Ty could attest to that.

I closed my eyes and decided that from there on out, I would be okay. I could handle whatever came next. Mom was right, I needed to rest and get better. I didn't know how long I would be in the hospital so until I left, I just needed to heal.

CHAPTER TWENTY-SIX

THREE WEEKS HAD PASSED, and there I sat in my car outside of *Brise*.

I had skipped my last preseason game, but started the regular season off with my team the best I could. I went to practice and talked to the media, but they were not yet aware of what I was dealing with off the field.

Things were easier since I knew Giselle was okay.

Coach had kept tabs and checked in with her, and he relayed back to me what he could. She had been shot in the leg and ulti-mately, that meant *Brise* was closed down. Usually in the morn-ings, I would pretend I needed donuts, and sit in the park, watching the door. Nothing ever happened, though.

She never showed up.

Neither did Mike.

The cops were still looking and investigating everything but they had pretty much believed what I had told them about my brother being involved. At least, I assumed they did. They still poked around and asked questions, but since I had nothing to hide, I never shied away from helping them.

According to the detective, Giselle never mentioned my name

at all. She told him we had been exercising together, like normal, but I had gone outside to talk to my brother. That was all she remembered.

It was the fact that she refused to talk to me that kept them lurking. He wanted to know why I considered her my girlfriend, but she refused to acknowledge it. Was I stalking? Obsessed?

Fuck, I didn't know what they thought, but I was sure I was going to get in a ton of trouble if I kept showing up to *Brise*. Especially at night, the way I had decided to do.

The blinds were closed but I could see the movement of shadows. Something in me had finally snapped because I got out of the car and walked up to *Brise*, anticipating the door being locked, which it was. I could hear the kids inside and Giselle clapping at them to keep practicing at home.

In a few minutes, that door would be unlocked and the kids would be leaving, and in that small window of time, I had a decision to make.

Did I risk pushing her away by going against her wishes? Or did I show up and let her know I was fighting for her?

Just as I heard the door unlatch, I backed away and waited for everyone to leave. Some of the moms recognized me and I nodded with a small smile. As always, Sam and Mrs. Watson were the last to leave and Sam ran to me, hugging me.

"Hey my man. How are you?"

"I'm okay," he was smiling but shrugged.

"How're things at school?"

"Ugh, still the same. Mom said I can quit dance after the recital. I have fun here, but I don't want to be picked on anymore."

My heart broke a little and I squatted down, even though Sam was tall and it wasn't necessary.

"Do you want to dance?" I asked.

"Yeah, but I don't want to be 'Sparkly Sam' for the rest of my life."

"Dude, dancing is fun, and you are so good. Don't let insults change who you are, or what you want to be. Because they're probably just jealous that you're so talented."

"I want to be tough like you," he said. "I'm gonna play football."

I shook my head and smirked, looking toward the ground before I looked back into his eyes.

"Wanna know why I come here so much?"

"Because Miss Metro?" He asked, smiling at me knowingly.

"Yes, that too," I nudged him. "But also," I lowered my voice because I was about to reveal a huge secret and I wanted him to know how much it was impacting me. "Twice a week, I come here and take ballet lessons."

"What? You dance?"

"Psh, you know it. And I love it. It helps me play better. And more than anything, I have learned that dancing is tougher than football. You have to be stronger than strong and super special to be able to handle dancing."

"Is that how you caught that touchdown against Seattle last week?"

Shit, Sam was on top of things. "It helped. Miss Metro taught me how to *assemblé* and I got both feet down in the end zone."

"I cannot wait to tell the guys at school," Sam laughed. "I bet they think you're too cool to do ballet."

I didn't even flinch. That was exactly what I wanted him to do. What did I care if a few middle schoolers laughed at me? At least they would be laughing with Sam and at least they would realize that dancing didn't mean you were weak or wimpy.

I stood up and nodded to a smiling Mrs. Watson. "Oh hey. How is your son?"

Her face fell, knowing I was asking about Reggie, and she shook her head. "He left the hospital, and got right back on the streets."

"I'm so sorry."

"I'm just going to pray and pray, Mr. Black. It's all I can do."

I thought about my brother for a minute. He was in a shit storm and if he wasn't dead yet, he would be, or in jail. Especially if he lost a hundred thousand dollars worth of drugs. Truthfully, I wasn't a praying man, but as a sentiment, I guess it was all I could do as well.

I hugged them both before letting them go, hoping I got to see them again soon. Depending on how things went with Giselle, I wasn't sure I would be back. I was going to do everything I could to let her know how much I cared about her, but who knew how she was feeling.

Trying the door again, I pulled, noticing it was unlocked, and I was kinda upset she hadn't locked it. Why did she always forget to relock it?

To my surprise, Giselle was prancing gracefully on her feet back and forth. After a gunshot, you would think she would be down a bit longer or at least have a limp. But she was as graceful as ever.

She looked different in other ways though, I just couldn't pinpoint it. Of course, her back was to me so I hadn't seen her face yet.

Clearing my throat so she knew I was there, I watched her elegantly turn around. A hand flew to her mouth and her eyes widened.

There was no scream but it was almost a complete reenactment of the night we met. Only that time, it wasn't Giselle. It was an older, but just as beautiful version of her.

"Where's Giselle?"

"Who are you?"

"I'm Ty Black." I swallowed because something about her made me feel inferior. Like I wasn't even in the same league, much less the same playing field. Where Giselle was poised and professional, this woman exuded sophistication, refinement, and elegance on a whole other level.

"Ty?" She smiled. "So you are Ty."

"Heard of me?" I smirked, but tried to keep the cockiness out of it.

"My daughter spoke of you," she glided to me and raised her hand for me to shake. "I am Galena Metrovik, Giselle's mother."

Her hold on me was firm and powerful. She looked a lot like Giselle, even the same slim frame and petite stature.

"Where's Giselle?" I repeated.

"Home," she held my eyes without elaborating. She was extremely intimidating. I understood everything Giselle told me about her, and just like Giselle, I had no idea how to navigate our conversation.

"I knocked on her door a few times," I admitted. "No one ever answered."

"Yes, I know," she backed away and kept tending to the things she was doing before I got her attention. "We hid behind the couch the first time."

I looked up at her words and she winked at me, a small smile tilting the side of her lips up. Instantly, I felt more at ease. Galena had jokes, and Giselle had obviously been talking about me more than just who I was.

"I'm not sure how much longer I can stay away from her."

"Honestly, my dear. I am not sure she has much resistance left in her, either. Why she is even fighting it, I have no idea."

Now I was smiling, bright and almost joyfully bouncing on my heels. "She talks about me?"

"Constantly," Galena said without even looking my way, almost as if it annoyed her.

"What should I do?"

"I am filling in for her while she is down. She is not to even attempt putting weight on her leg for another week, and after that, who knows. With that being said, at some point, she will return to *Brise*."

"So? I should wait on her?"

"Precisely. You must understand, Mr. Black. She thought you were part of all of this. Before that man hit her, he told her you were a part of it all. She saw you laughing outside with the first man who had broken into her business and hurt her."

"But I didn't…"

"I know that. She knows that now. But she wants to have a clear head and a forgiving heart when she sees you. Even if you were not involved, your brother was, and she has to be able to get past that."

Grunting, I placed my hands on my hips and tried reconciling what Galena had just said. It wasn't too hard, though. Giselle was hurt, physically and mentally. We were barely even starting things up together. Who was I to be needier than she was?

"Okay. But expect to see me here everyday, Galena."

"I would expect nothing less, Mr. Black. In fact, I have an excellent idea."

giselle

I DIDN'T SPEND the whole month in my apartment.

Occasionally, I made my way to the rooftop and watched the city go by. Thanks to the elevator and my fancy wheelchair, getting up there was easy. The space was designed for entertainment and enjoyment for the tenants, so it was a safe place for me to relax and think about things.

My mother had moved in with me temporarily and took the guest room without complaints. Then she asked me if she could take over my classes at *Brise*. She hated kids and reminded me often. Even some of the evenings when she got home from teaching my kids.

Yet, she went back every day and saw to it that they could practice for their recital. I was handling the books from home and networking with the receptionist over the phone on the accounts and backend of things.

We had costumes to order and bills to pay. These were things that I wasn't very good at, but was learning a lot with my mother taking over the actual teaching for a while. I even made a few contacts that were going to help me organize the business side of things better.

Since my mother was helping keep it alive, I had decided I didn't want to let *Brise* go. In fact, I wanted to expand and get more help there with me. The value of another teacher to help was proving to be invaluable. I would be able to add one or two more classes and on top of it, I wanted to use ballet to help other athletes the way I had Ty.

I might not have been able to use his name as a launching pad but Mr. Peyton assured me he had plenty of other players that needed the same type of help. So once a week, I would have a class for athletes and it would curb the enjoyment I found in using ballet for another platform.

"Darling," my mother called as she entered the apartment. Living with her there was no different than when we lived in New York. We fell right into the same routines we used to have.

"In here," I called from the dining room.

The chef my mother had hired was serving warm plates on the table with something for the strict menu my mother ate from. I just ate what she ate since I was never too fussy with my meal choices.

She waltzed into the dining room and took her seat, dressed in her usual perfect pantsuit and her hair done up to perfection. After each day, and unlike me, she took the time to change in my office after classes. She hired a driver to take her around the park so she didn't have to walk home—both for safety and to prevent perspiration. She wasn't too keen on the September heat in Atlanta.

"How was your day," she asked, placing a napkin on her lap.

"Good, actually. I got a lot of work done. Even ordered the costumes we picked out."

"Excellent!" She clapped her hands and smiled brightly. Galena may not like kids, but some part of me felt like she was finding enjoyment from the experience. Just like when I was a kid, she enjoyed teaching someone how to dance.

"How is Sam?"

"Sam is as amazing as you told he was. Absolute perfection."

My pride for him wanted to burst. If only he knew he had just been beyond complimented by someone with the highest standards in the industry. "See why I wanted to help him? Keep him?"

"Absolutely and darling, I think he will stick it out. I really do."

"I hope you're right," I chewed a full bite before I spoke again, not risking chewing with my mouth open in front of my mom. "Now we need to just sell some tickets to our recital. I thought about sending flyers to the schools the kids attend. Maybe we can get some of them to come?"

"Actually, I think that is an excellent idea. I also have a little plan of my own that may help as well."

"What's that?'

"Oh, it is a surprise."

Oh no, Galena didn't do surprises.

"Are you coming to our studio rehearsal next week? It will be our only one before we move on to the next act."

"Yes, I'll be there. I want to see the kids so much."

"Good. Now, tell me what else we need to do before the December show. It is only 8 weeks away, darling!"

I was putting weight on my leg and walking, though my limp was still present. I had been lucky the bullet didn't hit bone or any arteries, so it was just my muscle that needed to heal.

On the day the kids were doing their first act rehearsal, I climbed into my mother's car service and rode with her to the other side of the park. She was more surprised than I was at how well I was walking. Far from dancing, but walking well enough to get around without assistance.

Still, we agreed that I would sit in the office during the day classes, and get some work done. Then, when she was ready to present the first act, I would come in and watch inside the studio.

In my office, I quickly noted that there was not a thing out of place. My mother had not come in and messed with anything. It was actually a shock.

It was one thing to fuss over me after being shot, but it was another to take over everything that meant anything to me and not change it. She didn't even criticize me for things she would have done differently.

Several nights, we spoke about a mother getting a call that her child had been shot being the single most life-changing and eye-opening thing to ever happen. It made me think of Mrs. Watson the night we were at the game, and being there with her when that call came in, I saw firsthand what happened to that mom.

They do what they have to do. They cry, panic, get strong, cry some more, and then move forward to take care of them. That must have been what happened to my mother. The fear of losing me changed her.

Not entirely.

She was still the fabulous Galena Metrovik. She could still dance circles around me and anyone who dared to try. She was putting up with the kids at *Brise* but she hadn't converted to actually liking them. Her poise was still spot on, elegance was still intact.

I was told that I could be intimidating, but then, when people met Galena, they realized I was just a puppy. I wondered what the mothers at the studio thought of her. Maybe a mix of awe and fear.

Making calls was the first thing I needed to do in the office. The theater I booked, which I now regretted, was still worried about their loss of ticket sales hosting a child's ballet class. Even after I told them Galena Metrovik would be there, they still wanted more from me.

Getting comfortable in my chair, I logged into my computer but there was a folded piece of paper taped to my screen.

Opening it, I realized it was a handwritten letter. To me.

Giselle,

It has been six long ass weeks and I miss you so much. If you thought time would change things or make things disappear altogether, you thought wrong. All it made me do is want you more. Please call me.

Ty

He was right. Things didn't change where my feelings for him were concerned. I didn't regret pushing him away for a while, though. His brother was involved, we had unspoken things going on between us, he was in the spotlight all the time, he was trying to have a good season, and I wanted to let my life sink in. I wanted to be sure that any decisions I made were not a result of him.

So, I flipped the paper over a million times before grabbing my phone and sending me him a text.

I miss you too.

Not even a full 30 seconds went by before he responded.

Oh shit it worked.

I couldn't help but laugh at him. I pictured him looking at his phone and dropping it because I had risen from my secret cave and actually reached out.

Today is the first day I have been able to think clearly and move forward. It is the first day I don't want to hide.

Can I just say one thing?

I promise, swear, vow, take an oath, anything else.... I was not a part of Mike's plan. I had no idea what was going on, and he made a fool of me by making me let my guard down.

I know...

I know you thought I was a part of it. I know that it is why you pushed me away in the beginning, and I don't blame you at all. I just wish we had gotten a chance to talk.

We will. I promise, vow, cross my heart.... We will talk this all out and decide where to go.

I will call you when I get home tonight.

Promise?

Yes. I want to see you but I know you are busy. I have been watching the games, by the way.

Have you seen me dance?

Every week, Mr. Touchdown Man.

You ain't seen nothing yet....

I closed my phone and shook my head at him and myself. I missed him so much. I was so thankful he was patient and waited on me. His timing was perfect because I was beyond ready to move forward.

I moved along with my day, tending to everything I needed to do. I even had lunch delivered and ate a huge sandwich with greasy fries. My mother tsk'd at me for that, like I had said, she wasn't an entirely new woman. I just shrugged and told her I felt like celebrating.

Later that evening, the advanced class showed up and Mom told me to wait in the office while they prepared everything. I could hear the giggles of the kids and my mother telling them where to stand. That meant the door was open to the studio because if it had been closed, I wouldn't have heard much.

Finally, Mrs. Watson popped her head into the office and asked for a minute with me. She rounded my desk and hugged me, letting me know when she heard the news it was like hearing another one of her kids being hurt.

I asked about Reggie, but she didn't want to talk about it. But she did tell me that she had made herself the unofficial door locker when she came into the studio, so that she knew everyone had that barrier of safety.

Guilt that I never told the parents coursed through me. Just another one of my failures and being too worried about the loss of income from fear. Yet, it was also a learning experience for me and one I would carry into the next chapter of running *Brise*.

Mrs. Watson's phone chirped after a few minutes and she looked up. "They're ready for us."

I tilted my head and smiled. Must have been some production to have her back there to stall me and then get me out there on time.

I waved off her offer to help me walk and made my way into the studio. The parents were all seated behind the glass and the door was still open, most likely so they could hear the music during rehearsals.

Mrs. Watson led me to a chair inside the studio and told me to sit down. As I got settled, I looked around and noticed the accordion walls that mom must have moved into the place. The kids were all behind the walls and I knew it was supposed to help them mimic the curtain on the stage.

My mother waltzed out and presented the class to me before

taking her place next to me to watch and guide them as they went.

The music started and what I thought was going to be a Christmas jingle was replaced by a guitar and notes I didn't recognize. I cringed a little, realizing mother did in fact redo some of the performance I had already started.

It was okay, I took a deep breath and knew that she had every right to make whatever changes she needed to make. It was her show and if she wanted to change something, so be it.

Once the kids were all out and starting their first arabesque, movement from behind one of the accordion walls caught my attention and a man in tights jumped out in what ended up being an unremarkable jette'.

The surprise from him coming from nowhere had me scooting my chair back but it only took me seconds to recognize Ty. He was in all black—compression tights with suspenders. I'm sure on a normal man, the tights were supposed to be to the ankles, but for Ty, they were mid-calf. He wore a black t-shirt under his suspenders which wasn't typical but it was clearly a decision he made for modesty around the kids.

My jaw was dropped open, and on the floor. I watched on as Ty did a series of moves that I had taught him, and a few I hadn't. Peeking up at my mother, she was smiling and had her fingers circling, reminding the kids to pirouette.

When my head stopped shaking and the shock of seeing Ty wore off, I realized that the music playing was the same song we slow-danced to in his apartment. The only difference was, there were no lyrics, just music to the tune.

Ty continued to dance behind the kids, looking awful but doing his best. The parents were all smiling and seemed like they knew this was going to happen. To top it off, my mother must have choreographed the whole thing.

Tears started prickling at my eyes, the moment almost too

much for me to handle. I had so many questions and almost couldn't wait for the music to end so that I could ask them.

As the music started slowing down, Ty and Sam took center-stage and did a *brise* with their back feet extended and lifted perfectly. I definitely hadn't taught Ty that, and although I had worked with Sam on those, he had honed his skills in the past few weeks.

In the end, Ty lined up with all my little dancers and took a bow, making me shove to my feet faster than I should have to give them a standing ovation. Luckily, my mother was beside me and grabbed my arm for balance.

She leaned in and whispered to me.

"Did I ever tell you how much I loved your father? That I tried to find him?"

I looked at her with shock in my eyes. She never spoke about my father. I knew his name and knew their story but that was the extent of it.

"I should have never run away from him," she finished, before walking away to congratulate the kids.

Ty approached me and smirked, taking my hands in his. "I got awesome, right?"

"How? When? What?" I still wasn't sure which question I wanted to ask first.

He pulled me into a hug and whispered into my ear. "Let's get out of here and talk."

"I can't, the kids have to…"

"Nah, that was it. They're going to keep practicing, but this was my show tonight."

"I cannot believe Galena went along with this."

"Shit, it was her idea," he pulled back and looked at me. "I stopped by one night to see if you were here, and she had this fucking brilliant idea." He rolled his eyes and waved his hands in the air. "She was all like, 'Dahhhling, I have a brilliant idea.' And my dumb ass was like, 'What?' So yeah, here we are. Been here every night for three weeks to practice, well unless we were out of town for a game."

"How did you know I would answer your note today?"

"I didn't care, that was just a bonus. I was going to show up and show you my dance no matter what."

CHAPTER TWENTY-EIGHT

AFTER GISELLE SPOKE with all the parents, she and I left *Brise*. Galena had made me promise not to let Giselle walk too far, so once we were on the sidewalk, I scooped her into my arms and walked across the street to my car. I had managed to throw a hoodie on over my suspenders but from the waist down, I was in ballerina tights, out in the open for anyone to see and laugh at.

It didn't even faze me. I had my girl in my arms, and I was the happiest person in the world, tights or no tights. But I was still glad we were on the quiet side of the park. No one needed to see me in ballerina tights.

"I can walk," Giselle giggled.

"I promised Galena you wouldn't walk too much, and she scares me."

Her head fell back, laughter taking over her entire body. She could laugh all she wanted, but it was true.

Instead of taking her home, I took her to my place. We sat on my couch after I poured us each a water, quietly looking at each other. The moon was shining bright, giving me enough light to see her smile, the creases next to her eyes, and the way she bit her lip.

"I loved your song choice," she started, looking at the spot we danced in my living room all those weeks, shit months, ago.

"It's an important song," I shrugged, picking at the loose lint on a pillow where her feet rested. "That was the song that was on when I realized I had fallen in love with you."

Her breath hitched and her hand went over her heart. Her mouth was open and her eyes were glassy. She wasn't surprised that I loved her, but she may have been shocked that I opened with that.

"I know we have a lot to talk about but first thing's first. I love you. I have since before everything went to hell. Before you were hurt. Before we spent all that time apart. I told you, I don't blame you for needing the time, but at that point, I was already yours. The time away didn't erase it. Just made my feelings more evident. I needed to give you the time you needed and then dance my way back into your life."

"Before everything happened that night," she smiled. "I wanted to get home and ask you what we were, what this was that was happening between us. But I never got that chance and I was scared. Scared you were involved. Scared you would break my heart. Scared that as much as we cared for one another, you would always have your brother's back the way you told me he always had yours. I needed time to sort that all out."

"I know, baby. I know."

"It's been six weeks and the police haven't been able to find him. They told me you have been cooperative. Mr. Peyton told me how you were feeling, and I knew in my heart how true it was. I don't regret taking the time I did. I needed it. But I'm glad you came for me and didn't give up. I love you so much, Ty."

Other than Mike, I never knew what it felt like to be loved. But what I felt for Giselle was way beyond brotherly love.

"I'm working with the cops to find Mike. We will find him and he will be locked away for what he's done to you."

"I'm so sorry you are having to go through this, Ty. As hard as its been for me, I know you lost your brother in all this. I'm so sorry I couldn't be there for you when you needed me. I just—."

"Stop," I cut her off, not wanting guilt to be something she dealt with. "I wasn't alone. I had Coach and spent a lot of time with your mom. My teammates were filled in on what was going on and had my back. Cam even spent a few nights here at the apartment with me to make sure I was good. So I was ok, I promise. I had family with me."

Family wasn't always the people we were related to. Sometimes we tried so hard to hold on to our blood because we thought they were the family that would always be there. But through it all, I realized that real family was who you chose to have in your life. People you chose to love, not because of obligation but because you wanted to.

Giselle and I talked for a few more hours before I carried her to my bed. With her leg still healing, I knew I had to be careful. But nothing was going to stop me from feeling her tight pussy wrap around me.

"I missed you," she moaned as I slid her clothes gently off.

"Oh fuck, Miss Priss. Not half as much as I missed you."

"Did you…" she trailed off, turning a soft shade of red.

"Did I what?" I knew what she was asking, but I wanted to hear her say the words. I wanted to know that even after all our time apart, my uptight ballerina could use dirty words when she was with me.

"Did you… make yourself come?"

"From the moment I first felt that tight cunt of yours, it's been the only thing I want wrapping around my cock. Not even my hand and my imagination was good enough. I tortured myself. Waiting for the day when I knew I could fuck you again. So no, I haven't, which means you gotta go easy on me tonight. One touch from you and I may not be able to keep myself in control."

My lips were close to hers as I hovered over her body so I didn't give her time to answer. I pressed my lips to hers and pushed my tongue into her mouth. We had kissed all night, but that kiss was different. It was the one that I held onto as I pushed inside her body. We moaned around that kiss. We made love with that kiss.

Not until I was close to coming did I end the kiss and move my lips to her cheek and chin, down to her neck. As much as I wanted to kiss her, I wanted to hear her moan my name even more.

"Let me hear you, Miss Priss. Let me know how you're feeling."

"I feel so good, Ty. I missed this, I missed us. I was so stupid to push you away. I…"

"No baby, none of that. We are together now. That is all that matters. Now let me hear you moaning my name. Come for me because I'm about to fill your pussy up."

"Oh God," she cried. Her core started to clench and I hissed, feeling her body contract around me. "Ty!"

"That's right," I whispered.

My eyes were squeezed tight and it was the closest I had ever come to crying. Knowing we were finally together again, she was safe, and I could love her this way for as long as she'd let me was consuming me.

Giselle's nails dug into my back and I felt tingling down my spine. Another cry from her made my movements get jerky, and I growled as I released inside of her, just like I told her I was going to do. Filling her up, weeks' worth of pent-up need for her consuming us both.

It felt as though I would never stop, but maybe it was because I didn't want to. Even knowing my body was spent, I didn't want to stop loving her and feeling connected.

When I finally stilled, I looked down at her. She ran her hands over my cheeks and smiled but didn't say anything. She was happy, and I was a part of that. Never again would something stop me from making her smile the way she was right then.

"Your 'after sex' glow is still just as amazing as I remember."

"It's the glow I get being with you."

The rest of that night was spent laying in each other's arms. It felt like a beginning for us, but it also felt like the end.

The end of ever wondering what my life would be like without her, without love. The end of ever letting anything come between us. The end of her ever being hurt, sad, broken, or scared.

All I had left to do was make sure Mike got what he deserved.

giselle

ONE MONTH LATER

IN THE WEEKS that had past, Ty and I became a constant in all facets of each other's lives. I attended his games and he spent time at *Brise*. We mostly stayed at his place since my mother was still in town and living in my apartment, but we were always together unless he traveled for a game.

Though Mr. Peyton was no longer paying for Ty's dance lessons, we still spent time after the late classes dancing. Mom would go home, and Ty and I would carefully ease my leg back into motions that I was scared I had lost forever.

The doctor had cleared me for full range and I was going to physical therapy during the day, but nothing beat dancing in my studio. Especially with Ty.

I couldn't get him to wear the tights again but he no longer shied away from practicing ballet moves. He even told the media he attributed his newfound skills to ballet dancing with his girl-friend. When I was back to full speed, Mr. Peyton had already lined up another player for me to help as well. Though, Ty threatened the poor guy, telling him he'd kick his ass if he so much as looked at me wrong. He meant it too, and Mr. Peyton warned Ty that he would be traded or benched if he started shit for no reason.

His jealousy should have bothered me a little, but it didn't. It felt good being loved to the point of madness. To know that someone loved me so fiercely that they would risk everything they had worked so hard for to keep me theirs.

"What ya thinking about?" Ty asked as his hand roamed up my arm and to my shoulders. We were lying in his bed, soaking in our last hours before he had to leave for an away game.

"Us," I said simply.

"Good stuff?"

"It's all good stuff," I smiled. "But I need to be thinking about that recital. The theater is still giving me problems. I swear I'm booking a traditional theater for next year."

"Even after your mom and I both announced that we would be in the damn show?"

"Apparently you two are not big enough to be considered the level of celebrity they thought I promised."

"The fuck? Should I be offended? Because I am."

I nudged him and laughed, "Maybe."

"What about if we sold tickets to the football team? I bet every motherfucker would pay a lot of money to see me in tights."

"You would do that?" I raised up and looked at him with excitement in my eyes.

"Make a fool out of myself in front of my teammates to ensure that the theater laid off your back and the kids had a great show? Yeah, I would."

"What about football?"

"It's a Thursday, we will have practice that afternoon and then the guys can go to the show."

Tears pricked at my eyes and my heart felt so full. Ty told me every day that he loved me, but it was in his actions and ideas that showed me how truly loved I was.

In the middle of the night, I was startled awake. I sat up and looked around, searching for anything that could have woken me up. Ty was still asleep next to me and didn't seem to hear anything.

A few minutes later, I still hadn't heard anything so I got up to use the restroom before going back to sleep. I didn't bother with closing the door or turning on the light.

Just as I was about to head back to bed, the door to Ty's room burst open. I was too stunned to scream and when I realized what was going on, I hid behind the wall of the bathroom until I knew what to do.

"Bro, wake up." It was Mike and his voice was strained, in pain. "Ty, please."

Ty shot up and looked around, getting his bearings about him before realizing Mike was standing over him. He reached for me on the side of the bed, but I wasn't there and his face was panicked. But I knew he would want me to stay hidden, so I did.

"Mike?" Ty jumped to his feet and started toward his brother, concern for him replacing his panic for me in his features.

My heart broke just a little, seeing Ty still soften when it came to Mike. He was his brother, and I knew he loved him, but some dark part of me wished Ty would kick him out, hurt him, do something to rid us from ever having to deal with him in our lives.

Ty hadn't spoken of Mike much, but with him missing and unable to be located by the police, I knew he was worried. He wanted him in jail, but not dead.

Mike opened his jacket and it was then that I realized Mike was bleeding. It looked to be a gunshot but I couldn't tell in the dark space. Ty flicked on a light and started panicking, looking for something to help.

"Where's Giselle?" He demanded.

Mike was shaking his head and looking at him like he had lost his mind. "Fuck I don't know. I need help man. Please help me."

I still remained hidden, unsure what I should do. I was scared it was all a ploy to get Ty's defenses lowered. For his sake and mine, I needed Ty to keep thinking I was gone. His concern for me would keep him vigilant around Mike.

"What happened?" Ty asked, wrapping a sheet around Mike's midsection.

"I never found those fucking drugs," Mike snapped. "They've been hunting me for three months. What the hell do you think happened?"

Ty drew back and cocked his head. "They found you?"

"Yeah they found me, and they're still hunting me. Won't be happy until I'm dead. You owe me bro, you owe me big and I'm cashing in now."

"How the fuck do I owe you?" Ty shouted.

"I could have killed your girl but I didn't." I gasped but Mike was talking too loud for me to be heard. Ty's body started shaking and I knew he was tempted to hurt him even more. "I told Marc not to put a bullet in her because she meant something to you. I did that for you. I should have, I could have written her off as the one that had those drugs but I didn't."

"Marc is the one that shot her? I thought you said he and Dev left?"

"Fuck man, you couldn't handle our lives and you had to be thrown off the scent. You were busy being a ballerina and being softer than I had ever seen you. If I didn't get you off our asses, there's no way I would have been able to make the bank I did in this town."

"Giselle was shot, Mike. So tell me again how I owe you?"

"Yeah, I told Marc not to put a bullet in her, but you had to go off and punch him that one time and he was still a little mad about that. Can you blame him? He didn't kill her, though. Didn't even try."

"So you come in here thinking I'll help you because I owe her life to you? You think you can disappear and come up in here, leading God knows who to my doorstep, all because you think you did me a favor?"

Ty's voice was menacing, not loud but deep and I wondered if the devil himself had made his way into Ty's soul. Ty shoved Mike down onto the bed, blood seeping through the sheet Mike had around his waist as he fell.

Climbing on top of him, Ty started punching Mike's face, yelling and for a minute, I really was sure Ty would kill him, or let him die. That was something he'd never be able to live with and I knew I had to stop him. For as much as I wanted Mike out of my life, I didn't want Ty to suffer in any way.

"Ty, stop!" I came out and my words caught Ty's attention. He immediately stopped hitting Mike and jumped up, running to me.

"Baby, where were you?"

"I was hiding in the bathroom," I confessed quietly. Ty started to reach for me but there was blood all over his hands so he stopped. "We need to call the police."

Ty nodded and pointed to his phone on the side table, suggesting I make that call while he kept an eye on Mike. Mike was moaning and rolling back and forth in pain, but I could tell he was about to get up and make a run for it.

"How could you do this to me?" Mike moaned to Ty. "I'm your brother. Your only family."

"No," Ty shook his head and pushed Mike back down, making him work again to get up if that was what he was going to try doing. "My family are the ones that guided me to a better life, like Coach. The ones that had my back when I needed them, like Cam. The ones that love me despite the fact that I don't deserve them, like Giselle. You are my brother by blood and that's all. Don't say I never did anything for you. Because you being my blood is the only reason I'm not going to kill you myself. It's also why I am calling the cops. Jail is safer than the streets, *bro*. So you're welcome."

Mike started laughing like the joke was on Ty, but he was losing consciousness and was beyond being able to run or even think clearly.

I made the quick call to 911 and then an additional call to the detectives that I knew had been looking for Mike. The rest of the night had been a whirlwind of cops and questioning. Mike had been transported to the hospital and was expected to be fine after the bullet he was sporting was removed in surgery. Eventually, he would end up in jail and according to the detective, Mike turned in his counterparts as well.

He and about six other people had been using the businesses to break into in a quiet and slow part of town. Their goal was to hide the drugs in plain sight, but somewhere the gangs in town wouldn't be able to find them. Then when it was time to deal, they broke back in and claimed their drugs.

The curveball for *Brise* was the night Reggie came to class with his mom and brother. Reggie was a young guy trying to be someone he wasn't, tougher than he was. Just like Sam almost did, Reggie was falling victim to the peer pressures and bullying that went on around him. It was hard being a good kid when you grew up in a rough part of town. A part of town where most kids started dealing and working the streets at such a young age.

Reggie thought finding the drugs was his chance to get on the good side of the guys that were giving him trouble, but all it did was lead to Reggie being shot that day we went to the football game. He had returned to the streets, once again trying to be more than he truly was at heart.

Ty was once that kid and he knew it was a hard place to climb out of. But Reggie and Sam had something Ty didn't—parents that loved them. So he told Mrs. Watson that the second Reggie got home, to send him to *Brise*. He told Mrs. Watson that he would get Reggie a job with the team and it could be just the launch he needed to want to stay on the right side of the tracks.

It made me fall in love with Ty even more, which in turn, made us feel unstoppable. Not just in our relationship but in every aspect of our lives. We were both going to be better people for having one another.

Together, we were going to work to help kids like Sam and Reggie. We were going to move forward and help each other excel at our businesses and jobs.

Together we would laugh. Love. Dream.

And dance.

giselle

TWO MONTHS LATER

"PLACES!" Clapping my hands, I urged the kids to stand on their marks as our final Christmas performance was set to begin. It was a short rendition of The Nutcracker and the only song that had the kids, my mother, me, and Ty on stage at the same time.

Dressed as The Sugar Plum Fairy, I took my position as well. Ty waited on the side, dressed in his tights and tunic, for his cue to join me as the Cavalier. We were going to dance a beautiful Pas de Deux, or at least I hoped so. Between football and his other obligations, Ty and I only had so much time to practice.

My mom and the kids would be on stage as "sweets," dancing around us. Hopefully, they would distract from the fact that Ty was shaking with nerves and fear. His eyes kept cutting to the side where he could see past the closed curtain, and I prayed he didn't run before it was time.

The entire Atlanta Jets team was in attendance, as was the entire Atlanta Kings, which was the baseball team. Even a few players from the Miami Inferno soccer team were in attendance since Mr. Peyton's brother played for them and was told about Ty being in a tutu.

On top of all the athletes, the parents were given the first rows and had filled them to the brim in support. My mother also had a few people come in from New York to see her perform.

It was a packed house for The Buckhead Theater, and they were pleased with the production we had brought to them. They had even offered us a spot for the following year's performances as well. However, I kindly declined. As much as I loved my mother and Ty being able to sell out a theater, it wasn't sustainable, nor was it what I wanted for the kids of *Brise*.

Once I can establish a bigger and long-term production class, I may consider a large theater again. Until then, I didn't need the added stress.

Finally, the curtain opened, and the music began. I started a few steps with the kids behind me and my mother to the side. Once it was time, Ty leaped onto the stage, and the crowd went into an uproar of cheers and laughter.

As nervous as he was, Ty danced the best he knew how, and kept a smile on his face. When we touched, I could tell he was still shaking with nerves, but he couldn't have been more professional, and my heart opened to him even more than before.

His arms, chest, and neck were lined with tattoos, his hair was buzzed on the sides, and he had more muscles than He-man. Nothing about him belonged in tights, yet he was dancing with me and looking at me like as if I were a queen.

When the song ended, he took his bows with me and the kids. The crowd was on their feet, and while I knew most of them were in shock to see Ty so studious, most of them had to have been proud of the work he put into his dance. I knew he did it to make me happy, and a part of it was for the kids, but he soaked in the love he got for his work, and I had never been prouder of him. Not even when he caught a touchdown and did a pirouette in the endzone.

After the curtain dropped, the kids were released to their parents. My mother headed out with her friends while Ty and I were supposed to join the teams at a Christmas party on the rooftop of the Omni Hotel. Before we left, though, Ty pulled me back on stage and into a small spotlight in the center. There was no music, but there was where we danced anyway, swaying back and forth while holding each other.

"What are we doing?" I smiled, then rubbed my nose against his.

"I just needed one more dance with you tonight."

"I think there is dancing at the party, right?"

"No one is going to see the way we dance tonight," he whispered into my ear.

He pushed and spun me, making me rotate back into his arms. Then he dipped me back, making me laugh. When I was upright again, he pulled at my hair bun, making my waves fall over my shoulders.

"I will never get tired of being the one that lets down your hair, Miss Priss. For the rest of our lives, I want you to come home to me and let me take your hair down."

"Is that your way of proposing?" I teased.

He wasn't fazed. Just shrugged and smirked. "Maybe."

"Well do you have a ring?"

"Not yet. But when I do, are you going to say yes?"

"Are you going to dance with me every night?"

"I'll do anything for you."

"Then why would I say no to that?" I laughed and shook my head, realizing how ridiculous we were. We had been together for three months, and it was too soon to be engaged, but I never doubted that I would marry Tyson Black one day.

Ty

IT WAS FOOTBALL SEASON, and Giselle was again closing in on her Christmas recital. It was the busiest time of year for us both, but we found pockets of time to spend with one another every chance we got.

I preferred keeping her in my bed with me most of the time. Which was *our* bed. Galena had decided to move to Atlanta to be close to Giselle and help at *Brise*, so Giselle gave her the apartment when she moved in with me.

We were a few weeks away from closing on our first house. Something bigger and safer. Something we could build a family in, and host Christmas parties if we wanted. With so much change coming our way in the new year, it may have been the wrong time to add more to our plate of decisions, but as we walked the botanical gardens, all lit up for the coming holidays, I knew it was the right time.

We had made our way to the center of the gardens, where a huge, decorated Christmas tree stood. An instrumental rendition of Silent Night was playing, so I grabbed her into my arms and started to sway her back and forth.

"This feels like the perfect place to dance," I spoke close to her ear, not wanting anyone else to hear me.

"You and I can dance anywhere."

We were the only ones dancing, but neither of us cared if we caused a scene. We were content as long as we were in each other's arms and moving to the music.

"Just think," I sighed. "In a few weeks, we will be in our new home."

"Wonder what our neighbors are going to think when they see me getting home in my tutu to my boyfriend with all his tattoos and mean scowls?"

I laughed because we were the epitome of "opposites attract" and had turned quite a few heads when we went out together. Being in a suburban home with nosy neighbors was going to be hilarious.

"I don't scowl," I assured her.

"Not to me, but you do to everyone else."

"You're the only one I care about. Also," I took a deep breath, not really having a solid plan but knowing I wanted to go for it. "What if you came home to your scowling fiancé, or better yet, husband?"

"Do you have a ring this time?" She teased, expecting me to say I didn't. Instead, I stopped dancing and took a step back, lowering myself to one knee.

"Yeah," I nodded. "This time, I have a ring. Will you marry me, Miss Priss?"

She nodded and whispered, "Yes," as her eyes teared up.

I slid the ring on her finger and stood up, twirling her in a hug. "We need to go home. I want to make love to my fiancée."

"Or," she giggled as we started walking quickly toward the exit. "*Brise* is closer."

"Fuck, I love you," I laughed and started running. "And I love those mirrors."

"And as much as I love when you go soft and gentle, promise me when we get there, you will show me our special dance."

She meant like the first time when I fucked her on the dance floor. It happened often enough that we called it our special dance. And it was my favorite.

"As long as I can pull that stick out of your ass and replace it with—"

"Hurry," she laughed, cutting me off and picking up her pace.

Giselle

We practically sprinted to *Brise* and locked the door with us inside. With no one there, and no danger lurking, we shed our clothes in the lobby, and Ty carried me into the studio.

Setting me down in front of the mirror, I grabbed onto the barre and eyed him behind me. My name was tattooed in the middle of his chest, around his heart, in a space he said he hadn't realized he had been saving for me.

As he moved behind me, so did my name, flexing on his skin over his hard chest. I couldn't help but hiss and moan, knowing he was mine. One day, I was also getting his name tattooed on me. It'd have to be somewhere discreet, but I wanted him to know how it felt to see his name on the body of the person he loved.

Taking his finger down my spine, I started to wiggle, anticipating him touching me on my clit. But as his finger lowered, he stopped at my tight, back hole and pushed gently.

"You ready to give me your ass?"

We had never even attempted that, but we often teased. The thought alone turned me on, and that time, instead of teasing him back, I nodded, taking us both by surprise. "Yeah. Maybe then you'll finally believe I don't have a stick up there."

He snorted, and I watched the humor in his eyes as he debated on whether I was serious. But as his finger lingered, I pushed into him. His eyes caught mine in the mirror, and he knew I wasn't kidding.

"Harder, Ty."

He started cursing under his breath, so low I could barely hear him. It was a war inside his head on whether or not he should.

"Come on," I urged. "Show me how it feels to really have something in my—"

"Fucking hell," he bit out. "Had I known you'd be serious, I'd have brought something to make it easier. I can't hurt you, though, baby."

"You're hurting me now, not giving me what I want."

He stroked his cock with his free hand and lined himself up to my core. He slid in slowly, and his eyes met mine again in the mirror.

"I'm not gonna hurt you," he shook his head. "But when we get home, I'm gonna take you here." He pushed his thumb inside of me, and it hurt more than I expected, making me cry out.

As his hips started moving faster, he pushed his thumb deeper, creating a double-penetration feeling that was almost too much for me. Tears sprang into my eyes, and my breathing got ragged. It felt so good, creating a spark inside of me without my clit ever being touched.

I was tempted to take my hand between my legs and push myself over the edge, but just the idea of being touched in three different places was enough to make my body sing.

"Oh God, Ty," I moaned, so deep I barely recognized my voice.

He kept his pace, not letting up until he was sure my body was spent. Then he removed his thumb and turned me around. "You like it in your ass?"

"I want more," I nodded.

"How come I'm not shocked you liked it so much? Is it because you're used to being full that way?"

"Whatever stick you think I had up my ass was only to prepare me for being with you. I want you in every way possible. I want everything with you."

He crowded in close to me and kissed my lips hard as he sunk back into my pussy. After coming, I was so wet that the noise we made together was almost embarrassing.

But before I could spend too much time caring about that, Ty lifted me from the barre and into the middle of the dance floor. My legs were wrapped around him, and he lifted me up and down, stroking his cock with my body.

"I'm gonna put a baby in you, Giselle. Just like this."

We had never talked about kids, and I had never wanted my own, but just him saying the words made me nod. Maybe I did want a baby. His baby. Knowing Ty would be the best dad in the world made those feelings even stronger.

My tits were pressed to his chest, and my arms were around his shoulders. I held myself close and started sucking on his neck and ear. "Give me a baby. Fill me so full that those pills I take won't even stand a chance."

"Fuck I love it when you talk to me like that."

"Only for you," I reminded him.

"Come with me. Let's make a mess on this dance floor."

His words were like a button, and once pressed, I came the way he told me to. My moans were muffled against his neck, but he let out a growl that echoed off the walls.

We rode out or climaxes together, then fell to the floor. It took us a minute to catch our breath, but then he turned his head to face me.

"For real?"

"I told you I wanted everything with you."

"Me too. Because I cannot wait to see you with a round belly and the world's best dancing footballer inside. Knowing I put him there."

"What if we have a girl," I laughed.

"Same thing."

Smiling, I shook my head and stared at the ceiling. We were just beginning what was going to be the best dance of our lives, and I had never been happier.

afterword

Fun fact: My brother was an NFL player (my favorite player ever, of course). He once told me about a player doing ballet to help his game, and I HAVE NEVER forgotten that story. My brother has no idea how much I took from him for this book (because he's not allowed to read my books)…even the football play that Ty tests Giselle with was copied and pasted from our text messages. So thanks, bro!

Anyway, when Ty ended up being a good dancer in The Love We Make, I knew it was time to send one of the players to ballet.

Hope you loved his story!

Dance the night away,

Katie

about the author

Katie is a hopeless romantic, a proud mother of two, a devoted wife, and a die-hard baseball fan. She resides in Florida where she loves beach days and boat life.

There is always more to a Katie Rae book than what you think! She loves making us think while also making us swoon. You always think you know, but you have no idea, and that is what makes Katie Rae books so special.

Join the fun in Katie Rae Reader Group and sign up for Katie Rae's Newsletter!

Also, www.katieraebooks.com is now LIVE. Check out extras, events, book information, signed paperbacks, and MORE!

also by katie rae

The GAMES Series (interconnected standalones)

The Games We Play

The Lies We Tell

The Love We Make

The Way We Dance

The Way We Fight

Men of the Military (complete standalones)

Ranger

Raptor

RECON

Rogue

Miami Inferno FC Series (Interconnected Standalones)

Reckless Goals

Scoreless Nights

Twisted Assist

The Boys of Summer Novella

Pretty Boy

Man of the Month Club Novella

Love Bites

Another One Bites the Dust

Silverbell Shore Series (standalone)

Now and Then

Co-Write with Zoey Drake (standalone)

Dirty Monsters